SACRED COUNTRY

The Secret of Rampura

PRUTHVI RAJA

notionpress.com

INDIA · SINGAPORE · MALAYSIA

ISBN 979-8-88749-985-7

Contents

1

1980, Mysore, Karnataka

It was a quiet night at the Kumar residence like most of them are nowadays. The city of Mysore was cold and calm that day especially as the Dussehra celebrations in the city grandly ended the previous night with the oncoming of Vijayadashmi, the last of the Dussehra nights. Inder Kumar, a tall and broad-shouldered man with fair skin and good looks was sitting on the porch of his house meditating. His daughter Lata glaringly watched him going after his routine meditation. Lata was seated in a wheelchair with breathing pipes to her nose.

After some time Inder opened his eyes and as he looked at his daughter, the calm from his meditation vanished and it was as if everything was coming back to him: the pain, the suffering his daughter had gone through all her short life. It'd been four years since Inder lost his wife in a car accident and since then he had been a single father with an ailing daughter by his side.

Trying to brush away the sadness within him Inder picked up a book lying beside, which his daughter knew well not to fiddle with or touch as he had warned her several times. As soon as he picked up the book Inder got lost in thought and shuddered at it. It was the book referred to as *The teachings and experience of Jonestown*. He still remembered the horrible night. The sheer horror of the sight that night was permanently etched in his mind. Bodies were lying everywhere on the floor. You could not walk a few metres without being tripped by a body on the floor. Yes, Inder was a disciple of Jim Jones, infamously called 'the brain and creator of the Jonestown massacre'. 918 people were a part of Jonestown and everyone was reported dead by suicide on November 18, 1978, except nine who escaped of which Inder was one.

He then shuddered for one last time before he tried to get out of his thoughts and came to the present with his daughter. "Lata, what do you want for dinner?" asked Inder. Lata replied, "Anything that does not have mushrooms in it." Inder was known for adding mushrooms to his cooking for almost every dish and hence replied, "Ah, trying to be funny, huh?!!" Lata replied with a peal of quirking laughter which made Inder happy and smile as well. *What would he not give to see a smile on his daughter's face,* thought Inder who went into the kitchen to cook. Lata waited patiently as she heard the sound of her father cooking in the kitchen and after some time, he returned with steaming veg biriyani which was his daughter's favourite dish. "This one does not have mushrooms in it; so, I think you will like it," said Inder to which Lata smiled and started having her favourite dish with great pleasure which was evident on her face. Then Inder turned on the radio placed on the pedestal close to him and tuned in to Vividh Bharati. For their pleasure that day, R.D Burman's hits were playing on the radio which happened to be Lata's most loved musician off late. Hits of Burman played one after the other as they enjoyed. After a few minutes Lata felt uneasiness and in no time started holding her throat coughing up her food. Immediately she fell off the chair gasping for air. Even with her breathing pipes, she could not breathe right then. Her mouth started frothing slowly as she tried to plead for help from her father. With all this happening to his beloved daughter, Inder didn't move an inch to help her. He sat still and calm as a cold stone just watching over his daughter slowly giving up on life. He closed his eyes and started repeating the words, "I'm glad, for she is one with the soul," as his daughter breathed her last.

$$2$$

2020, Bangalore

"Remember, people, the more we criticize the current government, the sharper is going to be our decline, and hence I would say to go easy on the criticizing front and let the government do its job with some backing from our side as a newspaper company." Mr. Charu Shekhar ended his presentation to his team of journalists as he said these words. Mr. Charu was the no-nonsense Editor-in-chief of the Kannada Times who just meant strict business with his subordinates. He wanted his company to be the best-selling newspaper in the state and would stoop to any level to achieve this, even if it meant having some soft corners for the ruling government of the time. Mr. Charu could not also be blamed for this as most of the print and media journalism in the state and the country was based on praising the ruling regime to achieve better sales and ratings for their 'business' as it is called nowadays.

The meeting ended with these words and as for the employees, some seemed glad it was done and everyone got back to their cubicles or stations as they liked to call them. Rahul was late for the meeting and hence missed it. As soon as he entered through the door of the work station Charu spotted him, a young and dashing man with long hair combed and styled to the back complementing a tall, lean body. Charu with great excitement called out, "Rahul, in my office now. You are just the man I was looking for in the meeting." Everyone in the office looked at Rahul and started giggling as they knew that he was going to get some 'late-for-the-meeting treatment' from the boss. Rahul took a long breath for a moment and went inside the boss's cabin. "Take a seat," said Charu and as Rahul took a seat he continued, "Look at this, this is going to be your next assignment. I want you to do a detailed investigation on this matter and prepare a thrilling article that no one would want to miss." Rahul looked at the pictures in front of him and it was the crime scene photos of certain murders. There were vicious images of bodies lying dead and Rahul quickly noticed that all these murders looked identical as they appeared to be deaths by poisoning. Rahul was the Crime News Editor-in-charge of the Kannada Times, a job which he took reluctantly in the initial stages of his career but had grown to like it as a profession as time passed. To his surprise, he had become quite good at his job and hence could make out the nature of these murders just by looking at the photos.

Rahul after looking at the photos analysed them and thought for a moment before saying, "I'll send Ramesh with the details and the photos to the spot to investigate immediately. This looks interesting." He continued, "By the way, where did these murders occur?"

"That is what I want to talk to you about. These murders have taken place in a small village called Rampura in this state." On hearing this Rahul was taken aback and shocked to some extent. It was as if everything came back to him. Before he could get lost in his thoughts he was interrupted by his boss's voice, "I came to know that it is your birthplace and hometown where you have spent your entire childhood. So I want you to head this one personally and want you in the village investigating and preparing the article. Ramesh can assist you at the place." On hearing this Rahul immediately got up saying, "Sir, with all due respect I have to decline this as I don't want to go to that place. But I can assure you Ramesh and his team will do a fine job with this one."

Clearly, the boss was not happy with the reply from Rahul and expressed his dismay. "You know that I'm retiring in a few months, Rahul, and this job may be the extra edge you may need to fill this place and my boots," Charu indicated by tapping his chair. Charu knew that Rahul was an aspiring man with a hunger for promotion at his job. After this, Rahul thought and closed his eyes for a moment and on opening, reluctantly took the photos and headed out of the boss's cabin. Mr. Charu like always got his way this time too and let a smile sneak out for his victory.

Later Rahul sat at his desk and typed Rampura in Google Search on his computer. As Google showed him images of Rampura it all came back to him. The trauma, the hard goodbyes, and more importantly the sadness resonating with the place and why he left it for good despite his family still staying there.

3

2020, Rampura, Karnataka

It was a fairly short journey to Rampura from Bangalore, around 160 km of well-laid-out highway other than the small roads once you reach the village. Rahul and Ramesh finally found the guest house they were supposed to stay in. It was a brightly coloured house with a distinctly large gate for a fairly small structure. They walked in through the gate and knocked on the door of the house on the ground floor. The door was almost immediately opened by a lady in a saffron saree and black cloth tied around the wrists of both her arms. She was in her mid-40s, tall with a thin build and a long face attributed to her. When she opened the door, it looked like she was already waiting for someone and was perplexed and surprised when she saw Rahul and his companion. It looked like she was waiting for someone else.

"Good evening, we are here to meet Mrs. Shailaja Gowda," said Ramesh as Rahul was still figuring out the outfit the lady was in.

"Yes, that would be me. Is there anything I can help you with?" asked Shailaja who was still looking like she was expecting someone, but definitely not them.

Ramesh replied, "Hello, I'm Ramesh. I spoke to you over the phone regarding a place to stay in your guest house."

"Oh yes, Mr. Ramesh, we were expecting you. Welcome. This is Suraj guest house. Can you wait a minute? I'll just get my husband to show you your room." Exactly after a minute, she returned with her husband who was wearing white pyjamas with a saffron kurta. He too had a black cloth tied around the wrists of both his arms. After exchanging greetings, he asked Rahul and Ramesh to follow him upstairs where their room was supposed to be. As soon as they started to go upstairs another woman who looked the same age as Shailaja came in through the main gate to which Shailaja gave the expression that she was the person awaited. This woman too had the same outfit as Shailaja. *Must be a religious group they are a part of,* thought Rahul. Mr. Gowda showed them to their room and exited. Rahul and Ramesh entered their room and Ramesh closed the door behind them.

Rahul was writing something required for his article by observing the photos he received from his boss. Ramesh was just lying on his bed when a thought occurred to him, "Rahul, why don't you stay at your parents' place?"

Rahul thought for a moment before answering that question and then replied, "It's complicated, Ramesh. I don't exactly have a good relationship with my family." Ramesh looked dazed for some time and then said, "So what? Do they not like you or something?" Rahul smiled to himself and replied, "No, it's just that I am not too fond of them and that house." Before Ramesh could ask further questions which Rahul sensed beforehand, he shut the conversation by saying, "Let's not talk much about me and my family. We are here to work and let's focus on that."

"Ok," said Ramesh and continued after some moments, "You know, I'm a journalist like you and shall figure out your family issues somehow or the other," smirking with a naughty smile.

"Suit yourself, buddy," said Rahul smiling. "But for now we need to visit the local police station for further details on this case." Ramesh agreed and both of them started getting ready to visit the police station.

LOCATION—POLICE STATION

A medium-sized, one-floor-only building lay in the middle of fruit and vegetable stalls. Some were selling flowers too. The building was quite new compared to other buildings in the vicinity and the board on the building read 'RAMPURA POLICE STATION'. A large gathering of media was lurking around the station. Rahul, who was standing at the entrance, thought that these murders in the village were going to be the next big thing for the media and news portals of the state, though he could not guess why. Ramesh indicated, "Let's go in, Rahul, before there is an even larger gathering or else, we won't get the resources required for the material early." He meant that the boss wouldn't be happy if other companies and media houses were the first to break and report the story with new findings and investigations. After all, they were here to write the most sensational and thrilling happenings of the case.

Rahul and Ramesh went in looking for the Inspector for basic questioning regarding the case. However, they knew he wasn't going to be an easy man to find and pick his brain because of all the attention the case got lately. Also, the case was still unsolved and the killer was still at large. So the police had enough on their hands already.

After waiting for an hour to meet the Police Inspector they finally got a chance to meet him. The constable had already warned them that it would take some time and waiting if they wanted to meet the Inspector. So after an hour, the Police Inspector's cabin door opened and it was a familiar face that exited the cabin. By the time Rahul could remember who that was, Ramesh whispered in Rahul's ears, "Sanjay Khadke, local MLA." You could see the type of behaviour the constables projected around him and guess that he was an influential man of great importance. As two constables escorted him outside to his car away from the media, another constable signalled Rahul and Ramesh to go inside the Inspector's office, which they did. But as soon as they entered the office Rahul was surprised and to be honest, shocked when he saw the tall, well-built man with broad shoulders and catchy eyes. The Inspector was surprised to see Rahul too. Rahul was just meeting the man who was his childhood buddy and could also be considered one of his few close friends in the village during his childhood.

Rahul and Surya were inseparable during their childhood. They played together, ate together, and studied together as well, though they knew well that the latter was only an excuse to play more. Rahul, after his father's death, didn't like hanging around his house much due to personal reasons and hence always used to hang out at Surya's place. Surya's parents were also very welcoming to Rahul and hospitable to him. Most of the nights after his father's death Rahul used to crash in at their house. So this was a bonded friendship until a tragedy stuck in Surya's life too which made Rahul leave the village for good.

There was an awkward silence that ensued as they walked inside the Inspector's cabin. Ramesh broke the silence, "Good evening, sir. We are from the paper Kannada Times. I am Ramesh and this is my editor."

"Rahul," Ramesh was interrupted in between by the Inspector. The Inspector glaringly looked at Rahul.

"Oh!!… Surya…what a surprise!" said Rahul in an awkward and somewhat embarrassed manner.

"Indeed it is. Finally, you have graced us with your presence, Rahul," Surya said with a smile and indicated Rahul and Ramesh to be seated.

After both of them took a seat Rahul replied, "Well, I see you have accomplished your father's dream. Finally, became an Inspector, huh? I'm happy for you and so have you made your father proud. I guess he must be happy seeing you in this uniform all day." Surya took a moment before replying, "Well he passed away seven years ago, Rahul." Rahul immediately replied, "Oh, I'm sorry, my condolences." You could see the remorse in Rahul's eyes as he said this. Rahul was privy to the death of a family member and this too felt like a family loss.

"Well, don't be. You were never around to know that," said Surya. Rahul could sense the taunt made at him indirectly and before he could say anything Surya continued, "Well, enough about me. I hear from your mother that you have become the Crime Editor of your newspaper. Congrats, man!! Seems like a great job."

"It is," said Rahul. "And that's what we are here to talk to you about. Ramesh and I are here to investigate and report the serial murders that have taken place in the village in the last two months and I would really appreciate it if you could…" He was interrupted by Surya, "Ah, ah, no, no, no, no, no… my friend, you are here to report, not 'investigate'. You journalists think that you are investigators in a case but the truth of the matter is your duty is to just stick to reporting and not cause any hindrances to the investigation by the police, which is our duty." You could sense the anger in the Inspector's tone. This was maybe because he was tired of dealing with journalists all day or maybe he was just mad at Rahul for leaving him alone in the village during his tough times. Rahul couldn't figure out which one.

Surya continued in the same tone, "If I'm being clear, we have nothing to talk about. Sorry for the disappointment but I have a lot of work to do."

On hearing this Rahul got up off his chair, not expecting the meeting to end this abruptly and quickly, and started indicating Ramesh to get up and take leave. As Rahul reached for the door he turned around and said, "Well, it was nice to meet you, Surya." Then Rahul and Ramesh exited.

LOCATION—A RESTAURANT NEAR THE POLICE STATION

Ramesh was waiting for his order as he was quite hungry after the journey and then the visit to the station. The restaurant was small and you could observe the cracks in its walls indicating this structure was quite old, if not to use the word 'antique', thought Rahul who was seated opposite Ramesh. The restaurant was mostly filled with media people, journalists and police constables interacting with each other whose voices filled the hall. However, there remained silence between Rahul and Ramesh. Ramesh broke the silence after some time by asking Rahul, "Seems like the Inspector is not very fond of you considering you know each other quite well."

"Well, you would be surprised," said Rahul, "We used to be the best of friends." "He didn't seem like a friend of yours least being a best friend," responded Ramesh to which Rahul again said, "This village has a history of breaking relationships and communities. You would be surprised, Ramesh."

"Why would you say that?" By the time Ramesh could listen to Rahul's reply the waiter arrived with the food. He served the poha and took his leave. Ramesh continued, "Well, you did not answer my question."

Rahul was about to have his first bite. "You know. Let's not get into the past for no good reason. We have come here to carry out our work. Let's do that efficiently as we are professionals and get the hell out of this place." Rahul knew there would be another question coming from Ramesh; so before Ramesh moved his lips Rahul interrupted by saying, "Now let's eat our food and try knocking a couple of doors around the victim's families."

"I don't think any of the families would be very welcoming to the media right now." Ramesh had heard the other journalists chatting with each other when they were waiting at the station. But Rahul with a strange sense of confidence took out a list he had prepared. Ramesh had been wondering what Rahul was writing at the hotel and now he understood.

"This is a list of all the victims involved in these murders and their addresses. I slipped a 2000-rupees note to one of the constables while waiting and got this information from him."

"Well, I don't think it's of much use because none of them is going to be talking to us journalists after these poor villagers have received the media frenzy."

Rahul turned the sheet of paper towards Ramesh and pointed at a name on the list, "She will."

"Why her? What's different about her?" asked Ramesh.

Rahul took a brief moment and then said haltingly, "Well, for starters, she's my mother."

4

2020, Rampura, Karnataka

It was half past three in the afternoon when Surya returned home for lunch. He got out of his Mahindra Bolero and walked through the door into his house. The house looked traditional, which was common in houses built in this part of the state. He removed his boots and was above to go into his room when his mother called for him from the kitchen, "Son, you're back. First, have lunch and then go into your room." She had heard the sound of his vehicle coming in through the gate. Surya's mother Sharda was a stout, short woman who always wore a cotton saree. Perhaps she had lost the joy of a colourful life after her husband's death. Her hair had slowly turned grey. Even after her better half's death she always took care of her son and took a great interest in his life, as any other mother would do.

Surya, listening to his mother, sat at the dinner table and pulled out a file from his bag. Even after he checked out of work for a break, he could hardly let go of it. And to have a high-stake case with the media involved, any officer would be hard at it, least of all, a hardworking, honest officer like Surya.

His mother brought food and kept it on the table. But Surya was still glancing through his files. Looking at this Sharda snatched away the files and kept them on the sofa. Surya knew well not to argue and just ate the food that was served.

While eating together, mother and son usually talked about their day and this time it was Sharda who started, "So listen, I just got a great marriage proposal from a family in Bangalore. The girl looks pretty and has done her law degree. I hear she's even trying out UPSC. What do you think?"

"I think I have told you a hundred times and will tell you the same thing again, I AM NOT INTERESTED IN MARRIAGE RIGHT NOW."

"But you haven't even seen this girl," said Sharda.

"Mother, I don't think I need to. Can we stop talking about this?" said Surya firmly.

"Well, I was just trying to take your mind off the case. You don't need to be rude to me."

"I'm sorry, Ma, but I'm under a lot of stress regarding the case and it doesn't help that the media is all over it. And I haven't got much sleep lately."

Sharda's expression changed suddenly and she asked, "Why aren't you sleeping? Are those nightmares back?" It looked like she had touched a sore spot. You could see Surya hesitating to answer that. Sharda continued, "I can't help you if you don't tell me. Or… or… we can at least go to a psychotherapist for help. You know I may look traditional but I believe a doctor with ample experience can help you with this."

Surya now answered in angst, "Ma, I'm not having those nightmares. You can stop with your tradition and shrink bullshit. It's just that I haven't had time to sleep with the case and all." Before his mother could say anything, he washed his hands and stormed into his room.

As soon as he entered the room, he took off his shirt. Unlike his colleagues and counterparts, he was well-built with broad shoulders and chiselled abs. We could tell he would look after the physical aspect of his job well. Then he just crashed onto his bed without even changing his trousers. That's how exhausted he was. Slowly he began to fall asleep. After some time we could see his eyes fluttering.

A child was playing cricket on a muddy ground. The batsman hit the ball out of the ground into what seemed like a cut-down forest. The child went into the woods to pick up the ball. As he went deeper into the woods, he felt someone was following him. He turned several times to confirm but found no one. He eventually found the ball and as soon as he bent over to pick up the ball, he felt a powerful force grab him by his back. Before he could turn around to have a look at this force, he felt a pinch on his neck which made him unconscious. He then woke up in the back of what seemed like a store of some kind and as soon as he woke up, he saw a person covered in a black boilersuit and wearing an animal spirit mask which terrified the guts out of him.

Surya then woke up all sweaty and panting from his nightmare. His forehead was dripping with sweat and his palms were sweaty too. He tried to get a gasp of air desperately. After a moment he recovered from his nightmare and looked at the alarm clock lying on his bed table. It was already half past six and he was supposed to be back at the station. He got up off the bed and splashed water on his face in the basin. Then after putting on his shirt and adjusting his hair he took off as work called.

5

2020, Rampura, Karnataka

"Will you, for God's sake, tell me what's happening?" said a confused and rather shocked Ramesh after hearing that one of the victims of these serial murders was in Rahul's mother's house. He continued, "Is anyone from your family a victim in this case?" Rahul knew that he now had to come clean about this issue with Ramesh or these annoying questions would never stop. "The first victim, in this case, is our househelp Chotu. I realized this first in Bangalore when the boss showed me the pictures. I was taken aback when I first saw his body in these images. Let me tell you about Chotu *aka* Parag Bahadur. He is a Nepali boy. His father Lal Bahadur had been working in our home as a household helper. Soon Lal Bahadur died of a heart attack and Chotu was left an orphan as his mother had passed away long back. He had no relatives or family left in Nepal too. Hence my mother decided to take him in as one of our own and he replaced his father as our househelp. We grew up together as kids. My old clothes, toys, etc. were his. So yes, in short, my family was the only one he had left of him. Are you clear now?"

Ramesh finally found some clarity on this. Meanwhile, Rahul stopped a rickshaw and told the driver an address after which he and Ramesh got in. Ramesh had some more questions regarding why Rahul hated coming back to his village but knew well not to ask with the rickshaw driver present.

The whole ride till their destination was filled with silence apart from the noise of the old rickshaw engine. Soon the rickshaw came to a halt and both of them got down. Rahul was paying the fare when Ramesh was shocked to see a huge bungalow in front of him. It was painted white with ceramic tiles floor next to a beautiful garden with a variety of flora to observe. Hands down this was the biggest house he had seen in the village which usually consisted of traditional houses. Ramesh looked at Rahul as the rickshaw took off. Rahul could predict what Ramesh was about to ask and he replied with a smile and said, "Yeah. We did well enough."

"No buddy, I think you did very well if not the best in this village," said Ramesh with an even bigger smile. Rahul ignored the pun. Then both of them began walking inside the gate towards the entrance of the house. While they were walking Ramesh continued with his questions, "So what does your family do?"

"My father made his fortune through almond agriculture which later became a tiny business empire of its own. After his untimely demise my mother took over the reins of the business and she and my stepfather have been running it since." Rahul then knocked on the door as they arrived at it. It was opened by a young, pretty girl who looked like she was in her teens. Her hair was tied in a ponytail and she had particularly captivating eyes that Ramesh could not shake off. She was wearing a violet floral skirt. On seeing Rahul she was surprised for a moment and taken aback but eventually after registering the person who stood before her she hugged him. Rahul took some time but eventually put his arms around her and embraced her with reluctance as if it was forced because he had to reciprocate the love back.

"Brother, what a great surprise. I almost didn't recognize you. It's been years."

"Yes, it has been four years exactly since the last time I met you. My God! You have grown tall!"

"Yeah, and you have grown a beard. So it matches out." After saying this she giggled. And later she said, "Come, mother will be particularly glad to meet you after these many years. She misses you a lot, you know. There's not a day that goes by without her mentioning you." After saying this Tanusha welcomed both Rahul and Ramesh inside and closed the door after her. It was as if she did not register Ramesh at all in the presence of her brother.

They entered a large hall well-lit with the slanting rays of the evening sun entering through the large windows. Tanusha later went into a room on the top floor while Rahul and Ramesh got seated in the traditional, royal-styled sofas. After some time, a lady well in her mid-fifties and wearing a green sari came stepping down the floors into the hall and without any word came and hugged her son Rahul and later said, "Rahul, my son, I'm glad you have come. It's been such a long time. Everyone in the family missed you. Last I spoke to you on the phone was three months back when you had been promoted to Crime Editor of your newspaper." Kavita was a woman with a dominating personality. She had to be since the death of her first husband who had left her with a business empire to be taken care of. That incident had changed her from a loving wife to her husband and a caring mother to her son to a strong, decisive lady who demanded respect and admiration from her employees and labourers.

"It's nice to see you as well, mother. I hope you are doing well. I also hope Guru uncle is doing well." Guru Dutt was the name of his stepfather. Rahul never got used to calling him 'dad' as he called his own father. Guru was his father's friend who was widowed after his early marriage. Before he married Rahul's mother, he was a friend of his father and used to visit their home often. That time Rahul used to call him Guru uncle and that quite stuck on with him even after his marriage to his mother. Now Rahul was not quite happy with his mother's second matrimony which she did after a long period of dreadful loneliness and a lot of pressure from her family. Even though Guru tried to love his stepson and made efforts, Rahul never quite reciprocated it and never got adjusted to him. On spectating this, Kavita decided to have a child with her second husband but despite making many efforts they couldn't conceive a child of their own and hence adopted a daughter so that Guru could have someone to love of his own and could call his own daughter. Rahul, on the other side, rarely showed affection to his sister as well, in spite of getting a lot from her. But over time as he grew up he realized that none of it was anyone's mistake and fate had played a weird game with them. Since then Rahul was a changed man who, in spite of still not showing much affection to his family members, did have a lot of love and protectiveness towards them.

"He is the same son. You know, God has played a cruel game with him." As Kavita said this Tanusha returned with her father who was seated in a wheelchair looking crippled. She pushed the wheelchair and brought him to the hall. Ramesh was again surprised to see this. It had become as if his routine reaction by now. Guru had met with an accident soon after Rahul left the town to go to Bangalore. He supposedly tripped and fell down the stairs while coming down and injured his head badly. The doctors termed it as severe brain nerve damage and even after the best treatment his whole body was left paralyzed with him not being able to talk or express himself. As Kavita was not ready to keep him at a rehabilitation centre, she insisted the doctors on her taking care of him at home.

"Mother I have come here for…" and before he could complete his sentence Kavita interrupted him. "I know what you have come here for, son. First, let's have some coffee and then get down to talk."

"So what happened on the day Parag was killed?" asked Rahul after having his last sip of coffee. Kavita was surprised as he called him Parag rather than Chotu as he used to call him before. From Rahul's side, it meant strict profession and hence used the former name rather than the latter. Kavita took a deep breath and said, "All I know is Chotu left the house morning at the usual time and didn't return. By the time I woke up and realized that he had not been back, I already got a call from the police about his death and they asked me to identify his body."

Ramesh immediately asked, "Now what time did you say he left the house that day?" Kavita replied, "He usually wakes up by five to get fresh milk from Ramakrishna at his place." Rahul immediately started taking notes of this in his tiny notepad, though he already knew about this as it was the same time he had seen Chotu wake up and go for milk all the while he used to stay here. Rahul was not surprised that nothing had changed in the house as his mother did not usually take well to change.

Ramesh continued, "And what time did he usually return?"

"Ramakrishna's farm is around a 20-minute ride from here on a cycle. So he would be back by six usually unless he stayed a bit for a chat or two with Rama. Then he would be back within 6:30 or 6:45."

Ramesh continued, "Now this Ramakrishna. Did he know Chotu very well?" "Yes, Rama is famous around this village for his cattle and dairy. We have been going to him for ages. Rahul knows." Rahul gave a subtle nod in agreement and began to talk, "I guess you know the cause of his death?" Kavita replied, "Yes, they say it's a poisoning of some kind."

"It's ricin poisoning. All three murders that have taken place in this village are of ricin poisoning. Do you know anyone that would mean harm to him recently?" As Rahul asked this question, he knew the answer to this well. Chotu had no foes or ill-wishers as he was loving, caring and a standup man to everyone he met. Kavita replied the same. But this time she projected a hint of sadness and regret while speaking. It had been over a month since Chotu's death and as she spoke of him, the sadness and regret of losing him returned to her. Tanusha on seeing her mother on the brink of a breakdown started talking.

"The police have been investigating this case for over a month now and there have been 'no leads' they say every time we ask them. All we want is Chotu's killer to be caught and brought to justice. And I see the other families want the same too."

Rahul continued, "You need to understand that these processes take time and as far as I know of this case there have been a few suspects but none of them seems to have done anything because their alibi matches out."

Kavita spoke again, "It's ironic now that the police have now even started looking at these cases as suicide even if there is no evidence pointing to that. I mean why would a perfectly happy man with a happy life like Chotu even think of suicide?" As Rahul was sure that it was murder in all the cases, he and his mother also knew that 'the happy life of Chotu' was not completely all true. Everyone in the family knew that Chotu had certain scars from his childhood that no one including Rahul thought of mentioning right then.

Rahul later put his notepad in his pocket and got up getting ready to leave. Ramesh followed the same. "Ok, then. Thanks for talking to us, mother. We'll take leave now."

"What? Why? Just stay here. I know that we have had some differences in the past but you can still stay here anytime you want and for as long as you want."

"I'm sorry, mother. We have some work we need to get to but maybe another time." As Rahul said this you could see the disappointment on his mother's face. He bade adieu to his sister and stepfather on his way out. As they were leaving, Ramesh saw a maid folding out some saffron-coloured clothes and black wristbands made of cotton cloth. He immediately signalled Rahul to look at them. Rahul after taking a look couldn't wait more and asked his mother, "What are these clothes, mother? I have seen at least a few people wearing them in the village since I arrived." His mother's face almost lit up on hearing this and seemed that she was glad he asked this question. She replied, "Son, this is a gathering of a few people in the village. We share our problems, fears, sadness, feelings, and also our happiness and positive things happening in our life with each other. We help people get through tough times and it is guided by a Guruji named Vishwas."

"So you are in a religious group for old people," laughed Rahul.

"It's not a religious group. We are open to people from all faiths and all ages too. Your sister too has joined the group." On hearing this Rahul smiled at his sister rather too sarcastically. On seeing this Tanusha replied, "Brother, it's nothing too funny. It helps and guides people through their lives. You confront your deepest fears and feelings. Probably it's meant for you. You of all must try this." Kavita was glad to hear this idea and said, "Yes, son, you must definitely join us. We all would love it if you are part of our group. You'll look at life in a totally different way."

Rahul laughed again and said in a sarcastic tone, "Well I don't think so. I've done my share of yoga." Kavita and Tanusha knew that they could not convince Rahul and so he left. His mother was kind enough to give him a car to travel for as long as he stayed in the village. It was a Maruti Swift. As Rahul got inside the car only one thought was in his mind. He knew what his first article on these murders was about and it was going to ruffle some feathers in this village.

6

2020, Rampura, Karnataka

Rahul was seated on a chair on the balcony of his guest house. He seemed to be waiting for somebody. He had finished submitting his first article on the murders two days back and it was printed and circulated all over the state. He even told Ramesh to wait and watch what happens the next few days. Hence neither he nor Ramesh did any work for these two days. They were holed up in the guest house and whenever possible studying the proceedings of the case.

Ramesh came out to the balcony looking for Rahul and said, "I think he is not bothered by our article. It's been two days now. Maybe it would be best if we scout for another option." Rahul smiled and replied, "I think there is no man who is not fearful of their reputation going in the dust. He'll come around. Maybe he has not read the article yet." As soon as Rahul said these words, he saw the man arrive. The man he was waiting for these two days came in with a fierce motive in his eyes through the gates of the guest house. "There he arrives," said Rahul. He immediately heard the doorbell ring and Ramesh was surprised that the man had covered the distance between the gate to the door so quickly. *Boy! He must be really mad,* thought Ramesh. Rahul opened the door and Ramesh was absolutely right. Surya was mad as a bull seeing red, "What the fuck did you publish? Do you have any idea what you've done?" Rahul had written an article stating the incompetence of the local police in the village. He stated that the police were not onto any leads and mentioned that the police were looking to close off the case as mere suicides without any evidence because they could not solve these cases. And the article mentioned that in the centre of all this was the chief Police Inspector Surya Raj Honnal. "Well, tell me those aren't true," said Rahul.

"You have no idea about any of this," said Surya.

"I think I seem to have a pretty good idea if that got you here."

"I think you have crossed a line. I told you not to mess up with the investigation and stick to just reporting only."

Rahul answered with a smile, "Friend, this is reporting."

"Don't call me your friend. I think you lost the right to call me that a long time ago. We are not any fucking friends anymore."

Rahul closed his eyes for a moment as if to wash off his bitter words and then replied, "You cannot stop me from doing my job. I'll continue whatever I need to."

Surya muttered, "Bloody journalists. Fucking pain in my ass!!" and then turned back to leave the place as he knew he would land a punch if he stayed for another moment. But as soon as he began walking back he heard Rahul again, "Imagine, if I can make your life hell, I can make it a paradise for you as well. Something to think about." On hearing this Surya stopped walking and turned, "Now what does that fucking mean?"

"It means you help me and I make your life even better by helping you."

"How the fuck would you help me?"

"All I need is for you to share some details regarding the case and let me be a part of the investigation. You do that and I help you get a life upgrade." Surya with great disdain said, "What the fuck is a life upgrade? Rahul, are you trying to fucking bribe me? That's not going to end well for you."

"No, I wouldn't call it a bribe. That's too clique. I really mean a life upgrade." Surya had enough of this and turned back and started walking again when he was again stopped by Rahul, "Do you want to get out of this village for a better job?" This time Rahul seemed to have got his attention and desire for good. Surya turned around and looked at Rahul. Rahul continued, "I can write the articles in favour of you and your team as I did the opposite of it right now. I can make you look good. Sure, there is a promotion lying around the corner for you on the other side of this case. If not, I can convince my mother to get you into the good books of people running the administration in the state. Once you have the right influence you can go places. I know you want to serve the people of this village, but for how long? Wouldn't you like to get a promotion and get posted to a larger town or city with much greater pay and benefits? It's a better life for you and your mother, which by the way would surely make her happy." Surya thought for some time. There was an eerie silence. He was caught on the words of *'moving outside this village'* and that too for better pay and benefits, though, that did not matter much to him like the former. He also thought about how much Rahul had changed and just spoke and thought like a city fox. As soon as he came out of his thoughts he walked towards Rahul and looked him in the eye for a moment before extending his hand in honouring the deal. He then said, "See you at my place tomorrow morning sharp at nine," and then walked away. Rahul thought he had seduced Surya by tapping into his human trait of greed but Surya's reason for accepting the deal was totally different which neither Rahul nor anyone else could fathom. Surya always had a desire to move out of the village to escape his feelings and emotional scars but he knew well that his mother would not agree to move as her heart resided in this village. But moving out for a promotion and transfer of job would change the dynamics altogether and would be a good point to raise with his mother.

7

2020, Rampura, Karnataka

"Breakfast is ready. You people must be hungry with all the work. I think it's better if you people eat something and then get back to work." Surya's mother said this as she entered Surya's room where Rahul, Ramesh and Surya were studying the case files. Before anyone could reply she spoke again, "Rahul, I've made your favourite masala dosa. The one you used to like as a kid and would always ask from me." Rahul and Ramesh had reached Surya's house rather earlier than he expected them to. Rahul replied, "No, thanks, aunty. We'll have it later once we are done." Listening to this before she could reply she saw a stern expression on Surya's face that indicated her to leave the room now. Hence, not disturbing them further, she left the room. Ramesh, on the other hand, was starving and could easily go for a dosa but he controlled his desire by gulping his saliva back which had made its presence on hearing the words 'masala dosa'.

"So what we know of now is that all the three murders are from ricin poisoning," said Rahul.

"Yes," confirmed Surya.

"Ricin is a formula used by Soviets to kill their foes and also used to commit suicide by the KGB spies on getting caught," said Rahul, and before he could continue, Ramesh interrupted him, "But how did the killer procure it?"

This time Surya replied, "Though ricin is not available in India it is imported and procured illegally by terror outfits active in India. Also, there are reports that in the border regions of Punjab, packets of ricin are thrown by the other side from our not-so-friendly neighbours."

Now Rahul spoke, "All the victims vomited and then died of failure of kidneys, liver and the pancreas. I've also read that though ingesting a large amount can kill a person immediately, small amounts on the other hand can also take as much as a day or two."

"Now that's what has baffled the police," said Surya, "We don't have the most important fact about the time that they have ingested the powder. So the period in which the crime has occurred ranges a lot and hence makes it difficult to catch the killer."

"And the most important thing is why would anyone kill these people? You people have not even found the motive behind these murders," said Ramesh looking at Surya. Now Surya was enraged and replied, "If it's so easy, why don't you solve the case?" Rahul sensed the tension and before anyone could talk, he said, "Guys, we won't achieve anything if we start arguing and blaming each other. So, let's study this case in a different way."

"What do you mean?" asked Surya.

"I mean, instead of looking at a common thing between the victims, we should start looking at these murders one by one. The whole police force has been trying to look for something common to find the killer's motive, but what if we start analysing these murders as individual homicides and then join the dots to find the reasons behind these murders." Surya was impressed by this idea and also thought to himself about Rahul, *Gosh, he is good at his job* and said, "If we are going that way let us begin by studying the files of the victim Venkatesh aka Venky." And so the three of them started studying everything on Venkatesh. They had to study his whole life in order to find anything unusual.

After studying deeply for an hour and having discussions between them they found nothing. Surya was livid with himself and then said, "Bloody! His record is clean. I found nothing." Rahul replied, "Same here," and Ramesh indicated the same. Surya spoke again, "He has no prior crimes or complaints except a false complaint back in 2001 when he was 11." Rahul also had lost all hope but just for the sake of it asked, "What was the false complaint?"

"Complaint of being sexually abused as a child but it turned out to be false and the police closed the case stating the victim had made it up," said Surya. Rahul's eyes lit up as he heard this. Finally, he had found it. He had found the common thing between two of the three victims who were murdered. "Are you sure it was a false complaint?"

"Well, it's mentioned as a false complaint. So I'm pretty sure," answered Surya.

"I think we need to probe the complaint once again and talk to his family members," said Rahul.

Surya was baffled, "But why?"

Rahul replied, "Ok, listen. I didn't tell you this before but Chotu was also sexually abused as a child when he was seven. He had told us then but we never complained about it to the police as we did not find any sense in what he had told us." Surya and Ramesh's eyes also lit up now. Surya then said, "Ok, but what has that got to do with them being killed after more than two decades?" Rahul then got up and said, "The only way we find an answer to this question is by talking to the family members of Venkatesh and asking them about this alleged false complaint." He then walked out of the room. Surya and Ramesh looked at each other and then after a moment followed him out.

8

2020, Rampura, Karnataka

The noon sun was beaming down on the village of Rampura. It was 2 p.m. and it was lunchtime for most of the villagers. Surya knocked on the door of the house on whose gate was written Reddy Nivas. Behind him stood Rahul and Ramesh who promised to be mere observers and that would allow him to do most of the talking.

The door opened and a young boy who must be of age 8 to 10 stood on the other side of the door. Surya asked him, "Are there any elders in your house right now? If yes please inform them that the Police Inspector has come and wants to ask a few questions." The young boy without saying a word rushed back into a room and then after a moment or two came a man who must have been in his 30s. Surya recognized him as Venkatesh's brother Sai from earlier when he had first visited the family for questioning.

"So did you find the killer?" asked Sai rather with a firm, angry tone. Surya was disappointed with himself as he could not answer that question in a positive. But still, he swallowed his disappointment and said, "No. I'm not here for that. I wanted to ask a few questions if it's not a bad time."

"We already told you everything we saw and know of that day. What more is left?"

"No, this time I wanted to ask a few questions regarding the happenings of 2001," said Surya. Sai and his wife who had come out of the room now looked baffled by what Surya just said and Sai asked, "What do you mean?"

"Can we come inside and talk?" asked Surya. "And don't worry. These are a couple of my friends who are journalists and are here to help you. They won't bother you much and are here to just listen to what you have to say." The family who was in grief didn't care much about it and welcomed them in. Everyone came inside and got seated. "Thank you," said Surya.

"What do you mean by 2001?" asked a still confused Sai. Surya pulled out a paper that consisted of the false complaint made by Venkatesh and his father back in 2001. He handed it over to Sai and said, "What can you tell me about this?" Sai took a look at it for a moment and then replied with angst, "What does my brother's murder have to do with this? Is this some kind of game you people are playing? Huh? Can't you police just do your job for once?"

"That's what I am doing, Mr. Sai. We think this false complaint is a lead in this murder and can help us get close to the killer," replied Surya.

"But how does this matter?"

"I'll explain it later but for now I want you to explain and elaborate on this." Sai agreed to what he said and took a moment and then began, "My brother had come back home one evening after school and told us that he was physically and otherwise abused by a man on the way back. We immediately went to the police and described everything that happened to him as he told us. They filed a report and then after some days closed the case as a false complaint just because they were unable to solve it." Surya then asked, "Is there any particular reason for this?"

Sai replied, "They said the description of the attacker was made up and not possible. They even thought that my father had made up the event just to mess with the police and waste their precious fucking time."

"Can you describe the abuser for us?" asked Rahul who couldn't stay quiet no more.

Sai thought for a moment before replying to this but eventually decided to. "Yes. My brother said the attacker had a blue boilersuit on with a mask that looked like a goat's face. He couldn't recognize the person but came to know it was a male." As soon as Sai said this both Rahul and Surya were shocked and familiar memories came back to them though they were different from each other and of different circumstances. Rahul immediately got up and asked Surya to come outside for a minute. Ramesh followed them as he didn't want to be left alone with the family. As soon as the three were out Rahul had to confess something and he did. Rahul said, "Surya, I need to tell you something else too about Chotu's assaulter. Chotu described his attacker as wearing a red boilersuit of the same kind and a mask which resembled a lion's head. Though the colour of the suit is different and the mask worn by the assaulter is different, I think there is a familiarity between these cases and the sexual assaulter in both these cases may be the same man." Rahul had read Surya's mind. But for Surya the instance was different. It was not Chotu's case. It was something more personal. And to confirm this they had to visit the family of the last victim of these serial murders in order to find out if he had also been sexually abused as a child.

9

2020, Rampura, Karnataka

Surya was driving his designated Mahindra Bolero when Rahul who was sitting next to him in the front asked, "Do you at least have information on when or how these victims ingested ricin?"

Surya answered, "The post-mortem indicated that they all consumed ricin mixed with some food, though it does not indicate with what food exactly or at what time they were fed food with ricin. The time within which ricin shows its effect is immediately when consumed to two days of consumption, depending on the amount consumed. But the police did some work and collected all information regarding their food consumption and other activities which they did for the past two days till their death." Ramesh who was listening to all this while sitting in the back seat asked, "So did you find anything?"

"Unfortunately, no," replied Surya. He then continued, "We looked for all possible suspects and rounded them up too but we couldn't hold any of them as we did not have any evidence of any of the suspects having ricin on them. Many of them hadn't even heard the word ricin before and it goes the same for most of the villagers too."

Rahul then asked, "What I don't understand is how a poison and chemical which is used by Soviet-era spies lands up in this village and how did anyone procure this chemical without raising any red flags?" Surya then replied which was about to shock them, "As a matter of fact, according to our investigation ricin never came into this village at all nor did any medicine which contains ricin. And we have no leads of anyone manufacturing, producing, or cultivating ricin in this village too."

Ramesh was surprised and asked, "So how? Did ricin come out of thin air and land up in our killer's hands?

"Well, now you know why the police are unable to solve this," said Surya.

Before anyone could say more, they had arrived at Rehman Manzil, which was the house of the last victim in these murders. The last victim was Abdul Faisal Rehman, a famous painter who had fame in the state and was also awarded with coveted state honours. Abdul's fame was what got the media's attention to this case. There was a media presence already at his doorstep with two constables standing guard. As Surya got out of his car the constables saluted him and Surya along with Rahul and Ramesh began walking inside the house. The other journalists who were waiting out to have a minute or two with the family suddenly started talking among themselves when they saw Rahul and his assistant enter the house along with the Police Inspector. The other journalists seemed frustrated as they had to wait a long time before they could enter and even on entering, they were not sure if the family was willing to talk.

10

2020, Rehman Manzil, Rampura, Karnataka

"So tell me, Inspector. How can I be of help to you?" asked Irfa, Abdul's wife, after seating the Inspector and his friends in the hall of their house. The house looked like an art studio with painting replicas of Abdul's originals. He could not hang his own paintings for obvious reasons as they were meant for sale at auctions.

"I hope you don't mind: I brought a couple of journalists friends of mine. They won't be of much trouble as they are here just to observe and note down some stuff for their article and you can tell them when to stop if you are uncomfortable." Irfa looked at both the journalists for a moment as if to judge them and then replied, "It's ok." Surya continued, "So we are here to ask you about Abdul's childhood. Did he ever mention to you of being abused as a child?"

"What?" Irfa was rather surprised by this question. Then she continued, "What do you mean and what does this have to do with his murder? Surya then replied, "I know it's out of the blue but this may be a lead in the case and help us get closer to finding the killer."

"Ok. But what do you mean by abused? Because his Abbu and Ammi never even raised their voice against him. They were saint-like people."

"No… uh… I mean physically or even sexually abused by anyone outside as a child," said Surya.

"Listen, I don't understand what this has to do, but if you ask, in our four years of marriage he never said anything like this to me. And I'm sure he never said anything like this to his parents too. Insha Allah may their soul rest in peace."

After hearing this Rahul was rather disappointed as he thought he had already found a common thing between the victims and also he thought he was close to finding a motive behind these murders. But before they left Rahul asked, "May I take a look at these paintings if you don't mind?"

Irfa replied, "Sure, you may." And then Rahul, Surya and Ramesh took a tour of his studio and looked at some amazing paintings by this marvellous artist.

"There are some in his room too if you like to take a look," said Irfa who was proud of her husband's work and would not shy away from displaying it to anyone interested. And they went inside Abdul's room and spent some time looking at more of his paintings. After looking for a while before they left the room Rahul's eyes were caught by a small briefcase tucked under a shelf. "May I ask what is in that briefcase?" asked Rahul. Surya and Ramesh too had a look at it by now. Irfa looked at it and replied, "Those are some of his paintings as a child and teenager. He said he used to draw these based on the dreams and nightmares he used to have as a kid." Rahul got interested and asked, "May I have a look at it?" to which Irfa nodded her head and said, "Sure." Rahul then opened the briefcase and started to have a look at some paintings which looked amateur as it was drawn by a kid. While looking at the paintings one by one, he suddenly noticed something familiar. And he took a particular painting from below and he was exhilarated after looking at it. "That's it!! I knew it. Surya, look at this," said Rahul. Surya and Ramesh came forward and looked at the painting. Surya froze immediately after looking at it. It was a painting of a man dressed in a green boilersuit with a mask resembling the face of a wolf. Surya, Rahul and Ramesh were shocked at this sight. Rahul was right. But this affected Surya particularly and was even more personal to him. He then said to Rahul, "I need to leave. Sorry, but you guys catch your own ride back to the guest house." Rahul noticed Surya getting flustered. After saying this Surya immediately left and went down and sat in his vehicle. He now knew who was the killer's next target. It was none other than himself. He started the vehicle and left.

11

2020, Rampura, Karnataka

Rahul and Ramesh were travelling in the autorickshaw back to their guest house when Ramesh broke the long silence which had prevailed after Surya left. Ramesh finally asked, "Why do you think he left in such a hurry?" Rahul wished he had an answer to that question. But no one other than Surya had the answer to it. Rahul then replied, "I have no idea but what we know now for sure is the killer is targeting all the people in this village who were abused as children by the man in the boilersuit with the mask." As he finished saying this he was caught by the sight of a huge hoarding that had a huge photo of an old man, probably in his 70s with a long white beard and hair coming down to his shoulders. He was wearing a saffron robe and a black band made of cloth around his wrists. The sign mentioned "WELCOME" in block letters and also the date within which people could have a *darshan* of the Guruji. Guruji was staying in Rampura for the next three days after which he would continue his journey throughout the state 'healing people' as was mentioned on the placards and hoardings that lay within sight. Ramesh immediately asked the auto driver to stop as he had caught sight of someone familiar. He then told Rahul to look in a particular direction. It was none other than Surya's mother Sharda. Rahul said to Ramesh,

"You go back to the guest house and inform the boss about the latest findings and I'll follow you later."

"Why, where are you going?" asked Ramesh.

"I'm going to find out about Surya and talk to his mother. I think there is something fishy going on with him."

"Ok, then," said Ramesh after which Rahul got down the rickshaw and Ramesh indicated the driver to leave. Rahul then followed Sharda into the mutt. As soon as he entered the mutt he saw a group of around 50-60 people sitting in a large hall who were segregated from the other group of around another 100 people by a railing. All of them were wearing saffron clothes with black wristbands made of cotton cloth. He soon gathered a look around till he saw his mother Kavita standing in a corner and talking to Sharda. He then immediately started walking towards them and the closer he got to them he realized that Sharda was weeping and his mother was consoling her. And by the time he got to his mother, Sharda had left and sat in the second row among the people who were closer to Guruji.

Kavita on turning around was surprised to see Rahul attend the gathering. As soon as she saw Rahul she was glad and hugged him. She then said with an air of excitement, "Son, I'm glad you decided to come. I knew somewhere inside you wanted to come here but I left it for you to realize. And I am right, aren't I?" And before Rahul could explain the reason he was here his sight immediately fell on the bearded man who walked inside the hall from a room that seemed to be behind the hall. You could tell there was something charming about this old man as he captivated the attention of the whole hall along with Rahul and his mother. He was dressed exactly like in the hoarding. Rahul's mother immediately said to Rahul, "Son, have a seat in the back row. Since you are a beginner, you will have to be seated in the back rows. After some time and some more visits if you are lucky enough and catch Guruji's attention you will come and sit in the front rows." Rahul began to speak but was interrupted again by his mother, "Ok, son. Have a seat. Trust me, your life's going to change." After that, she left and sat beside Guruji on the podium. Rahul now realized that his mother must be a veteran around here to sit close to the leader. And as told, Rahul sat in the back row. Though he would not like to admit it, he was now all curious and wanted to know more about this gathering of people and his attention was more specifically grabbed by the leader or so-called 'Guruji Vishwas'.

Guruji held the mic and began his session. He said, "Now all of you can start greeting each other with warmth and a loving embrace. I want you to hug the person you're sitting next to." As he said this, people began hugging each other and the person next to Rahul, a middle-aged man balding with age, opened his arms widely to embrace him to which Rahul had no choice but to hug. He was reluctant though and seemed cagey showing some love for his fellow partner. He did not want to grab attention to himself by being the only person not to hug their partner. Then Guruji continued, "Let's start our meditation by listening to what I have to say. Everyone close your eyes and hold each other's hands." Guruji took a moment and a long breath and started speaking again, "What is God? There is no God. There is only love. Love is God. Love is a healing remedy. Today we are going to reach out to areas where man has some sense of difficulty. Today I'm going to feel something which secularists term as something paranormal." He then asked everyone to open their eyes but still hold each other's hands. Then he pointed to a lady sitting in the front who was old and seemed to have a problem with her sight. He then continued, "Ma ji, you have a problem with your sight. The doctors say you will lose your sight in a matter of days. Am I right, Kanaka?" Kanaka replied, "Yes, Guruji." Guruji then continued, "You are not able to see me right now. I know. You are not able to see the people that have gathered here today. I know. Your life is going to get much harder as time passes by. I know." Kanaka immediately started crying. Then Guruji got up and came forward. He then touched her eyes with his hands and covered them. Then he continued to speak, "Kanaka, what do you feel now?" Kanaka takes a long breath and replies, "I feel love." As soon as she said this the whole crowd went wild and started cheering for her and Guruji. Guruji then walked back to his podium and took his seat. He then continued to speak, "Remember, children of love. There is no creator. There is no destroyer. We humans were born by love, live by love and deserve to die with love eventually. We are not supposed to face suffering as the world does. All our sufferings will be healed by the one and only DATURA." He then indicates Kavita to bring something to him on which she got up and went to the room behind the hall and came back with a plant having white flowers. She kept it in front of Guruji. He then continued to talk, "Children of this world, hail Datura. The one and only solution to your sufferings lie in this beautiful plant. You worship it with full dedication, discipline and most importantly love, then take my word, there will be no sufferings for you. All your sins will be eternally forgiven." The crowd cheered once more and started chanting '*Jai Datura…Jai Datura…Jai Datura*'. Listening to the chants Guruji gave a wide smile of satisfaction and got up and left the hall back into the room through which there lay an entrance to another hall. All the members sitting in front of the railing followed Guruji to the other hall. This included Rahul's mother Kavita and Surya's mother Sharda. Rahul then got up to follow them when he was stopped by a guard. The guard said, "Please, sir. That's only for a selected few. You can stay in this hall itself where there will be a meditation session presided by one of Guruji's own students. He will also teach you about the importance of Datura as well as how to worship it." Rahul on listening to the guard went back but he had a glance inside the other hall and he spotted MLA Sanjay Khadke waiting inside for Guruji and his disciples from the front row. Rahul wondered. '*What has an MLA got to do with this Guruji and why is he here? Maybe he must be a follower of this Guruji too,*' he thought. Later Rahul didn't want to stay anymore and hence left the place. He came out and wondered if this Datura was the same plant he had seen at his mother's place. *Were they of the same plant?* he wondered. But without thinking about it too much he got back to the thought of the murders in the village and why Surya left immediately after seeing the painting. He had a lot on his mind than to worry about a Guruji and his followers. He thought, *'Well, this whole nation is a collection of different Gurujis and their followers,'* and smiled to himself. He then called for a rickshaw and left the place to head back to the guest house. From there he thought of going to the police station after lunch. Little did he know what awaited him there.

12

2001, Rampura, Karnataka

"Don't forget to get cash. We'll have ice cream today," shouted an 11-year-old Surya to Rahul who was supposed to get the bat and ball too. They had planned to play cricket that day as it was not raining anymore. There were showers throughout that week in Rampura. But that day it seemed like the Rain God had listened to the children's prayers and for sure they wouldn't want to disappoint Him by staying at home.

Rahul came out with a bat and a tennis ball. They got on to their respective bicycles and rode out through the huge gates of Rahul's bungalow. As they were about to hit the road they were stopped by a red Chevrolet which was taking a turn into the gate. It was being driven by the police officer Lakshman. Seated in the passenger seat was Sharda. As soon as they stopped the bicycles Lakshman said to Surya, "Son, take the keys to the house. We are going to the hospital. Just have to collect the results of a regular test. Your mom and I will be back soon." Then Sharda said, "Surya, food is on the table. So directly go home after playing and have it." Surya nodded in the affirmative. He thought to himself, '*Well they don't need to know my plans of having ice cream today.*' Then the car reversed and hit the road. After that, even the bicycles hit the road on the opposite side towards the *maidan.*

The two of them rode their bicycles at great speed. They zoomed past every tractor and animal-pulled cart. Though they had not decided to race each other to the *maidan* it was an unsaid thing between kids that age on who could ride their bicycles with great expertise and pace. As they were about to reach the *maidan* Surya heard a car pull up inside the forest which lay beside the *maidan.* It was a forest rich in sandalwood and previously had been the playground of many wood thieves who would come there in stealth to cut and loot some of it. But since the forest department had become vigilant as of late that would happen rarely. Surya wanted to have a better look inside the forest to see who it was but he was stopped by Rahul who now was at the gates of the maidan. "Surya, c'mon, what's taking you so long?" shouted Rahul from a distance. On hearing Rahul, Surya got distracted and got back on his bicycle and rode it inside the *maidan.* The excitement of being able to play after a week got over his curiosity.

It had been over an hour since they started playing. They were all tired except the batsman who was enjoying his time on the crease. The bowler, Rahul signalled to Surya who was fielding deep on the long-on boundary to come closer inside the circle to the mid-on position. Though they were mere children playing they gave importance to each match they played like an international cricket match as was the case anywhere cricket was played in India. So Rahul took his run up with great zeal and determination to knock over the stumps and bowled the last ball of his over. The batsman seemed even more talented and determined to hit the ball out of the park and that was what he did. The ball flew over Surya to the long-on position and then pitched and went inside the forest. Rahul was frustrated with himself now. Surya knew he was the one who had to get the ball from the forest as he was the closest one to it. Surya jogged tiredly inside the forest. He was greeted with the sound of crushing dry leaves under his feet. He had made a calculation as to where the ball might have been. But on reaching the spot he couldn't find it. So he looked around for a minute or two but to no avail. So he decided to go even deeper into the woods. He saw a large banyan tree in the middle of a bunch of sandalwood trees. When he approached the banyan tree, he finally found the ball lying on the other side. So he went to the other side of the banyan tree and bent over to pick up the ball when he felt a sudden force grab him by the back. Before he could even react to it, he felt a pinch on his neck which was actually a syringe injected into the back of his neck.

The next thing he saw when he gained slight consciousness was nothing. It was completely dark. He couldn't see a thing. He couldn't open his mouth as they were taped together. He tried to rip apart the tape on his mouth but then he realized he couldn't move his hands as they were tied together firmly behind his back. His shoulders were aching from the uncomfortable position he was lying in. He felt a bump here and there and hit his head constantly with a metal object. He then realized slowly that he was in the trunk of some car. Before he could react further, he lost consciousness again.

Surya's eyes slowly opened once more. He was barely conscious. He had a stinging pain in the back of his neck, probably because of the syringe being injected in a rush. He had a terrible headache. His arms were still tied in an uncomfortable position to the back. But the tape on his mouth had been taken off. He realized that he had been kidnapped but unfortunately, he couldn't make even the slightest sound as he had no energy left in him anymore. Then as he lay there, he felt someone touch his hands. Slowly his hands were untied. He tried to feel his hands by moving them but he was so tired and the blood circulation to his hands had stopped. Then he heard a person whisper in his left ear, "Shhh… don't worry, don't worry, I'm here." The voice was muffled because the person had worn a mask. The person then came in front of Surya. Surya mustered up all the strength he had and slightly lifted his head to see a man with a black boilersuit with the mask of an ape. Unfortunately, before he could find out more, he lost consciousness again.

Surya then opened his eyes again to a large banyan tree. He slowly tried to pick himself up. But his body was aching so badly that he fell to the ground to the sounds of crushing dried leaves. He tried to get up again a couple of more times until he successfully got up. He had a bruising pain on his right shoulder near the traps. He had to move his T-shirt to see the damage and it was bad. He had wounds on his traps from being carried in the trunk of the car. He also observed that his hips were paining a lot. He lifted his shirt up to see what had happened. What he saw was both confusing and terrifying to him. He had marks which looked like fingerprints all over his tummy and hips. He could see the colour change on his skin in these areas. Suddenly he was struck with a bolt of fear and he looked around him to find the assaulter. But he was relieved to find none. He then saw a tennis ball on the ground, when he looked around. He picked up the ball and ran straight towards the *maidan* with whatever little strength he had left. As soon as he reached the maidan he was greeted by an empty field. This scared him a little. But he soon realized it was dusk and all his friends including Rahul would have gone home. He wondered if they had searched for him. But it was not the time to think. He had to reach home as soon as possible and inform his parents. So he looked for his bicycle and was glad to see it in the spot he had parked earlier. He hopped on it and pedalled as fast as possible towards his home. He was afraid if the kidnapper showed up again.

Finally, Surya reached home. He wondered if his parents would be looking out for him. But he saw their car parked in the driveway. This indicated that his parents were home. He was glad. He came towards the door to find it half open. He pushed it and came inside. He was greeted by an eerie silence when he stepped in. Usually, the door would be locked from the inside and would only be answered by his mother on a knock. But this time it was different. He found it strange. He thought, '*If the car is parked here, it means that father is home.*' As he moved from the corridor towards the hall the silence got him a bit afraid. After what had happened to him it made sense to be a little paranoid. All types of thoughts raced through his mind. He wondered if something had happened to his parents. The fear kept on creeping at him slowly as he walked one step at a time towards the hall. He eventually reached the hall and was glad at the sight to see his parents sitting at the dining table. But they were not relieved or happy to see him, as any parent would if they knew their child was kidnapped. He then thought, '*Maybe they don't know I was kidnapped.*' But apart from that, they were seated with a genuine worry on their face. He even saw tears roll down his mother's cheeks. This got him worried and he came up to them and asked, "What happened, mother? Why do you look worried?" His mother held his hands and pulled him closer to her. She then slowly put his arms around him and hugged him. Surya now was getting worried and asked, "Can someone tell me what happened?" His mother told him to take a seat. She then said, "Son, your father has been diagnosed with bone cancer." He then looked at his father for a moment. He could not process what was happening. After all, he was an 11-year-old kid and you could not blame him after the day he had. He then asked his father, "So what does that mean? Are you going to die?" His father laughed it off saying, "Nooo... nooo... Your mother is getting worried for nothing. The cancer is detected at an early stage. I'm going to fight this. It's just a matter of days. Then I'll be fine. You'll see for yourself. And by the way, your father is quite sturdy and strong for him to be beaten by this. So don't worry like your mother." He then smiled at Surya and hugged him. Seeing the situations that had developed at home Surya decided not to bring up the subject of him being kidnapped. It would only worry his parents more in these trying times. Besides Surya couldn't even explain what had happened to him as he was unconscious most of the time.

As days passed his father's health deteriorated more and more and he couldn't bring up the subject. Days became weeks, weeks became months, months became years and finally, his father passed away. He could never find the right time to tell it to them. After some time, he learned to put that incident in his life as a nightmare. Whenever he would come to think of that moment, he would convince himself that it was just a nightmare. Guess he had found his way of living through it. After all, he thought, '*Life must go on*'.

13

2020, Rampura, Karnataka

It was 12:20 a.m. when Rahul took out the car given by his mother for a drive. At least that was what he said to Ramesh. He had told Ramesh to sleep the night as they had barely slept since they arrived. He told, "I need a breath of fresh air. Also, since my mother told me to visit her whenever possible, I think I'll sleep at her place for the night. She'll be glad." But Rahul had other plans for the night. He did not have an iota in his mind that wanted to sleep, especially after seeing how Surya had reacted and left them hanging after having a look at the painting.

Rahul thought he would visit Surya this past noon after lunch. But after lunch when Rahul had phoned Surya, he did not answer his call. Instead, he got a text from Surya asking him to visit him at the police station at 12:30 a.m. Surya had texted that he had something important he had to share with Rahul and had asked him strictly to come alone. Rahul wondered: *Why would Surya call me alone at this time of the night? Maybe he has something important to share regarding the painting he saw.* Rahul always thought Surya was a strange, secluded man, at least after his father was diagnosed with cancer. He would not talk to Rahul, avoid being together and always wanted to be alone. This was one of the reasons Rahul decided to leave the village as his only friend here had suddenly changed and would avoid him constantly.

Rahul had written a sensational article which would inform the readers of the latest developments in the case. He had confirmed in the article that the killer was targeting people who had been sexually abused by the man in the boilersuit. But before sending it to his chief editor he wanted to know more about the man in the boilersuit who he slightly doubted could be the serial killer too. Somehow, he had the feeling that Surya would know more.

So now Rahul was driving on the empty streets in the village. He just had one thought in his mind now. '*Why did Surya react the way he did after seeing the painting? Why has he called me alone? This was the same behaviour Surya had exhibited after learning about his father's cancer. But why would he react like this now? Surely there has to be something common between these two situations.*' Then suddenly a thought hit Rahul's mind like a bolt of lightning. *What if there really is something common between these situations? What if it has to do with the painting? What if Surya knows the man in the boilersuit? What if Surya was also sexually abused by this man? It would make a lot of sense, especially in his reaction after seeing the painting. It would make a lot of sense of his behaviour in his childhood after that incident. Maybe he wasn't shaken up by the news of his father's cancer after all. Maybe he was shaken up by being sexually abused as a child by the man in the boilersuit.*

It all started to make sense to Rahul now. He also thought that if that's the case Surya could be the next target of the killer.

He had to be warned. While thinking of these things he sped quickly through the deserted streets to eventually reach the police station.

He parked his car on the side of the street and got down. Then he started walking towards the main door of the police station. At the door, he was greeted by a constable who was already fast asleep sitting in his chair. There was no other individual in the station except this constable. So Rahul walked inside the door and started walking towards Surya's cabin.

He opened the door to Surya's cabin and he was shocked to see that no one was there. He looked around the cabin but to no avail. Rahul thought '*Am I late?*' and looked at his watch. But it was still 12:28 and he had in fact reached early. So he waited in Surya's cabin for a while. After a minute of waiting, he had the urge to use the loo. So he got up and went to the loo. But as soon as he opened the door to the loo he was shocked by the sight. But this time it was more tragic. There was puke all over the basin and below it, he could see Surya lying unconscious. Just one thought came to Rahul's mind and he knew that he was, in fact, too late.

2020, Rampura, Karnataka

Rahul stood by the parking area of the government hospital of Rampura. It was an empty field where people usually parked their vehicles if they wanted to visit the hospital. The field was visited occasionally by wild pigs and had its share of street dogs too. Rahul stood taking support of his car bonnet and lit a cigarette using the lighter that he had bought just a few minutes back. He was not a regular smoker and had left it for a while now but after what he had witnessed he thought he deserved one. So Rahul took a lungful of the tobacco smoke as if it included all his worries, anxiety and confusion and let it all out as he exhaled the smoke. This was his way of meditating as he was not one of the conventional kind.

Immediately after he took his second puff Ramesh came in from the hospital to the parking area where Rahul was waiting for some news. Rahul immediately asked, "So what's the news?" You could see him with great anxiety waiting for some positive reply. Ramesh replied, "The doctors say that he is currently out of danger, but the coming hours are crucial; so they are going to keep him in critical care for the next two days. He can come out of critical care if he responds to the treatment well."

Rahul took a big sigh of relief. This was marked by him taking another puff of smoke and letting it out signifying the relief he had just got on hearing the news. He was caught off guard when he saw Surya lying on the bathroom floor unconscious. For a minute Rahul couldn't process what had happened and how he could help. But after a minute he gathered himself and went near Surya to check his pulse. He realized that there was still a faint pulse he could feel. That well indicated to Rahul that he still had time. Rahul immediately woke up the constable guarding the police station and informed him of the situation and showed it to him. The constable too was shaken up by the events and being woken up from sleep to this situation didn't help him at all well. However, Rahul and the constable immediately picked up Surya and put him in the rear seat of Rahul's car. They drove down to the nearest hospital quickly as they could. It happened to be a government hospital. Fortunately, the current regime in the country and the same party government in the state which usually was targeted for bickering by the so-called woke liberals had actually done a good job when it comes to public health service. They had modernized the hospitals with good and latest pieces of equipment all over the state and would appoint only highly qualified doctors for the job. This actually saved Surya's life. Rahul wondered, what a difference good governance can bring into someone's life.

Ramesh then spoke, "So it means he was sexually assaulted too by the man in the boiler suit. Right?"

"Yes. But this time the victim is alive to tell the story. He can tell who poisoned him or what did he eat or drink last for this to happen."

Then again Ramesh said, "But it will take at least two days to get to talk to Surya. What if there are more people who have been sexually assaulted by the man in the boilersuit and if they are the next victims of the serial killer?"

Rahul replied, "Well we don't have any other option but to wait." He then continued, "But in the meanwhile, I could talk to Surya's mother and inform her about the incident. Maybe she has something to share."

So Rahul left for Surya's home from the hospital to meet Surya's mother. As soon as he reached Surya's place, he knocked on the door and also rang the bell a bunch of times. But it was all to no avail. There was no answer. Then he pushed the main door trying his luck and to his surprise, he realized it was open all this time. '*This was strange,*' he thought. '*Why would anyone in their right mind keep their front door open at this time of the night?*' Rahul then slowly and with stealth made his next moves as he began to walk towards the hall of the house. There was no one he could find. Then he moved to the dining hall and kitchen area where still no one was found. Rahul felt a little anxious again as he walked inside Surya's bedroom only to find Sharda lying unconscious on the bed with puke all over her. There was a teacup just beside her on the table which was empty. This suggested that she drank tea which had ricin in it.

So Rahul this time without wasting another moment went to Sharda to feel her pulse but this time, unfortunately, he was too late. Sharda was no more. The surprising thing was that Rahul noticed her having pictures of Surya from when he was a child to now in her hands tightly clasped.

15

2020, Rampura, Karnataka

"What time did you arrive here?" asked the presiding cop who arrived at the crime scene.

"Around 1:55 a.m.," said Rahul.

"And why did you come here?"

"I had come to inform Surya's mother of his condition. I thought she did not know of Surya being poisoned."

"And did you find her in this condition when you arrived?"

"Yes. She was already dead by the time I got here. I even checked the pulse and could not find any. That's when I called the cops," said Rahul.

The officer continued, "I assume you knew the victim well."

"Yes. I used to reside here and knew her well. Surya is my friend." It had been a while since he referred to Surya as his friend. He was submerged in a nostalgic feeling of being able to call him a friend again, even though Surya was fighting for his life at the hospital.

"Ok, I think I got all I need as of now. We will require you to visit the police station and give your statement later on. I think we are done here," said the police officer.

Rahul replied, "Thank you." As the police officer moved towards the body to inspect it Rahul had one last look at Sharda. At that moment a flurry of emotions rushed through him. The dominating emotion was sadness. Today he had lost someone who had been like a mother to him all his childhood. He remembered the times spent with her. The way she was hospitable to him when he wanted to get away from his own home and family. The delicious food that she had fed him all those years. The way she used to make up the bed for him when he stayed the night at their place. Her home and her heart were always open for him anytime. He regretted that he could not make up to her for all the love she showered over him.

As he turned and was above to move from the crime scene the police asked, "One last thing Mr. Rahul. Have you touched or tampered with anything around here?"

Rahul replied, "No. I knew well not to." Saying that Rahul turned again and left the crime scene and got out of the house where he saw tens of villagers waiting outside of the taped zone. They were all curious to know what happened. You could hear the murmurs between them. Rahul knew what was going to be the topic of discussion among the villagers for the coming days and perhaps months.

Ramesh was waiting for Rahul near his car. Rahul had immediately called Ramesh after he called the cops. He moved towards Ramesh when Ramesh said, "Are you alright?" Rahul nodded his head in affirmation but went on to say, "She was like a mother to me." Rahul was one for not expressing his emotions and here where Ramesh expected him to be shocked and grieved by the incident, he still kept his composure and kept his tears aback. Then there was a brief moment of silence until Rahul spoke again, "I don't know how to relay the news to Surya once he wakes up. She was the only person he had, especially after the death of his father." Then again there was a brief silence until Ramesh spoke this time, "On the phone, you said you needed to show me something. What was that about?"

Rahul replied, "Yeah. Get inside the car, I'll tell you." As Rahul said Ramesh got inside the car in the passenger's seat. Rahul got inside the driver's seat. Then Ramesh asked again, "So what is it?" to which Rahul turned back towards the rear seat and picked up a cup lying below. It was a green cup usually made for tea or coffee. Rahul then said, "Listen carefully, this is the cup in which Surya's mother drank the tea which I'm assuming had the poison in it." Before Rahul could continue further Ramesh said alarmingly, "Dude! You shouldn't have touched it. It is evidence of the crime. And in this case, going from your assumption it is the prime evidence. You need to give it back to the police." Rahul asked Ramesh to calm down and said, "Hey hey hey!! It is the prime evidence and that is why I'm not giving it back to the police. Listen, I sense something fishy with the investigation and forensics of the previous murders. I contacted a police friend in Bangalore and asked him to send this cup to the lab for testing in Bangalore. I think it may all make sense once we get the reports from Bangalore." Ramesh now seemed to get the gist of it and asked Rahul, "What do you want me to do?"

Rahul replied, "I want you to take the cup to Bangalore and give this to the police officer I'm talking about. I'll make sure you both get in contact. Once the results are out I want you to relay them back to me." Ramesh thought for a moment and then nodded his head in affirmation.

"Great. Let us get back to the guest house from where you can rent a car online and leave for Bangalore immediately," said Rahul, and then started the car and drove out of the gate which was now swarming with more and more people as time passed.

16

November 17, 1978, Jonestown, Guyana

Jonestown was a people's church congregation led by Pastor Jim Jones in San Fransisco. It included people from all races coming together especially black being the slight majority. This was rare, especially during those times when racism was still largely prevalent in American society. The church promised to heal the souls and scars of people. It also promoted something they termed **apostolic socialism.** However, Jim Jones was forced to leave the United States because of his ideology. Hence later he established Jonestown on agricultural land in Guyana where 918 followers of his resided along with him and his family.

Out of the 918 people, one was Inder Kumar, who came all the way from India as he heard about Jim Jones and his teachings. Inder had just lost his wife in an accident and his daughter was terminally ill. He had come to Jonestown believing in the promise of Jim Jones who claimed to heal broken souls and get people through tough times in their lives. From the beginning, Inder was fascinated with Jim Jones and his persona. He admired the way Jim captured the attention and imagination of his masses. Inder grew to admire him so much that he wanted to be Jim Jones himself. As days passed Inder became a close confidant of Jim and started to work as one of the security personnel to Jim Jones. Like other security personnel in the settlement, Inder was given a rifle, Glock pistol, and a Swiss army knife. Inder knew how to handle weapons from his service in the Indian Army before the death of his wife. This highlighted the paranoia under which Jim Jones lived especially since the U.S government was after him for human rights abuses and fraud.

So on November 17, 1978, Congressmen Lee Ryan of the United States arrived at Jonestown to look for himself about the whereabouts of Jonestown. He was sent by the U.S government to investigate Jonestown. He was accompanied by his team and a handful of relatives of the residents of Jonestown. After staying the night in Jonestown Congressman Ryan and his delegation were impressed with the activities in Jonestown. He saw that people were genuinely happy there. However, the next morning, the 18th of November, cracks began to appear in Jonestown. People residing there secretly confessed to Congressman Ryan and his team of physical, sexual, and mental abuse in the town. Some people even relayed their plans to escape Jonestown. Jim Jones caught ahold of this and hatched a plan. He sent Inder and other security personnel to drop Congressman Ryan and his team with some defectors back to the airstrip. But no one knew what was to happen there.

Jim had told Inder and his team to kill Congressman Ryan, his team, and the defectors before they could board their flight. As soon as they reached the airstrip Inder and his team started firing at Ryan, his team, and the defectors. This led to the death of Congressman Ryan, the defectors and some of Ryan's teammates. Only two of Ryan's teammates escaped alive into the jungle that lay surrounding the airstrip. Inder ordered his fellow assassins to chase them into the jungle and kill them while he himself thought, he should go back to Jonestown to update Jim on the situation and developments.

When Inder reached Jonestown he was shaken by what he saw. Hundreds and hundreds of dead bodies lay on the ground in such a manner that he could not walk a step without stumbling on the bodies. After a moment of thinking clearly, he knew what had transpired there. This was what the residents of Jonestown had been preparing for the whole time. They knew it wasn't going to happen like this for sure but they also knew it was a possibility. This was what 'white nights' were all about. When Jim Jones would hit the air siren in the settlement and call out 'WHITE NIGHT' on the speaker, the residents knew what it was. They would all gather around in the main town hall and practice mass suicide from poisoning. This was what had happened there now, only for this time it was real rather than practice. Everyone including children was made to drink Kool-Aid mixed with potassium cyanide. And those who resisted were shot dead by the people having weapons. Jim Jones shot himself in the head. A total of 909 people died that day in Jonestown by mass suicide. The reason behind this was Jim knew he could not keep his town for long as Congressman Ryan would inform the U.S congress of all the human rights violations in Jonestown and eventually the full force of the U.S Justice department would fall on his town and shut the town for good. This would also eventually lead to the arrest of Jim Jones and extradite him to the States. And Jim thought, '*If he wouldn't get to survive, then any of his followers also shouldn't get to.*' He had such a hold on his followers that they would die on his command. And that was what had happened here.

Inder thought of killing himself too by shooting himself in the head, but as soon as he put the gun to his head, he thought of his daughter who would be left all alone to die. He didn't want that to happen. So he escaped into the jungle from where he made his way to the city. From there he took a flight to the United States and stayed there for two nights before taking another flight back to India.

17

2020, Rampura, Karnataka

Surya lay on the bed sobbing in pain and regret. He had become conscious just this morning and was informed of his mother's death by Rahul. Rahul had prepared all these days on how to relay the heartbreaking news to Surya but couldn't find any way which would make it easier on Surya. Rahul slowly put his hand on Surya's shoulders and said, "I'm very sorry. I can't even fathom the pain you are feeling right now. I knew how much you loved her." Surya was very close to his mother. She was the only one he had especially after losing his father. Surya then said, "I need to go and see her," and then tried to get up from the bed but immediately fell back as he still did not have the strength in his body to pull himself up. Rahul immediately held his hand in support and said, "Surya, you are still not in a position to leave the hospital. They just took you out of critical care this morning. You still need to recover." Surya then replied, "What the fuck are you saying? My mother just died. How can you tell me to relax here while I still have to perform my mother's last rites?" Rahul wasn't prepared for this question. It was going to be the most bitter answer he must have given to any question in his life.

"Surya, your mother died three days back," said Rahul.

"What?" said a shocked Surya.

"Yes. Your relatives already performed the last rites."

"What do you mean? I'm her only son. How can they perform the last rites without me?"

"Surya, you need to understand. You were fighting for your life and death here. We were not even sure you'll come out of this alive. The doctors also informed me that it would take days before you gain consciousness and that too, there were slim chances of it." After hearing this Surya broke down again. He could not handle it anymore. The pain of losing a family member especially, a parent, was what Surya had experienced before but he did not expect the second one to be so sudden and could not fathom the possibility of not performing the last rites by himself. Then after some moments, Surya calmed himself down and said with a burning flame of anger, "I swear, whoever poisoned my mother, I'm going to put a bullet right through that person's head." He then continued, "It looks like the same person who poisoned the rest of the victims." Rahul then took a moment before he could say anything. What he was going to say was not going to be easy for Surya to listen to. He finally said, "Surya, I don't think anyone killed your mother. It looked like she took the poison herself. It looks like a case of suicide."

Surya replied, "What are you saying? Why would she do that?

"Listen, I'm not sure why she would do that, but I was the first to arrive at the crime scene and from my experience, it looked like suicide."

"Why do you tell?"

"I saw a cup from which she must have drunk tea before her death. It looked like she prepared the tea herself. There was no one at the house except her at that time. From the looks at the crime scene, I think it's suicide." Surya could not believe what he was hearing. So he said, "What rubbish. What did the police say?"

Rahul then replied, "The police could not find any evidence. They are still in the dark. The only thing they know is that she has been poisoned."

"What about the teacup they found? Isn't that evidence? You just said so."

"No, they did not find the teacup. I took it before the police could arrive. I have sent the teacup with Ramesh to Bangalore for examination."

"But why? Can't they examine it here? Rahul, you did the wrong thing by not giving it to the police."

"Surya. Just think for a minute. All these murders have taken place in the village and we still could not find any leads in this case. Hell, we could not find any source of ricin too. Don't you think there is something fishy? Let's just wait for the results from Bangalore to come back. We may find something. If not, there is nothing to lose."

Surya then thought for a minute and then said, "Ok. Let's try it your way." After that, there was a brief moment of silence before Rahul spoke. This time he had a question for Surya, "You were also one of the victims of sexual abuse by the boiler suit man, weren't you?" Before Surya could reply Rahul continued, "I know. You don't need to explain. I figured it out after your reaction to the painting. I also know why you didn't tell anyone, especially your family. I'm sorry I left during those tough times. But you need to understand, that you never shared anything with me regarding what had happened." Surya took a deep breath and then said, "I just couldn't. I just couldn't." Tears were rolling down Surya's eyes looking at which Rahul's eyes were filled. Rahul shut his eyes for a moment and tears rolled down his eyes too. Then Rahul gathered himself and asked Surya, "Who do you think poisoned you?" Surya replied, "I don't know." "What did you eat last?" asked Rahul.

"I didn't eat anything. All I drank was tea given by my mother that evening." Rahul was shocked after hearing this and after some moments Surya realized the unsaid thing too. He looked at Rahul and said, "Why would my mother poison me?"

"I don't know Surya. But later, she kills herself too. Something fishy is definitely going on in this village." Suddenly Rahul's phone rang. It was Ramesh. Both Surya and Rahul looked at each other. Then Rahul picked up the call. During the whole call, Rahul did not speak anything. He just heard what Ramesh had to tell. At the end of the call after some time, Rahul said on the phone, "Great work, Ramesh. You can come back to Rampura now," and hung up the call. Surya curiously asked Rahul, "So what is it? What did Ramesh say?" Rahul took a moment before saying, "The traces on the teacup indicate poison was in it. But, the poison is not ricin."

18

2020, Rampura, Karnataka

"What? What do you mean it's not ricin?" asked a rather baffled Surya who at this point had received a bunch of information that would leave any person of sane mind and character perplexed.

"I had my doubts and now it seems true," said Rahul.

"What are you talking about?"

"Listen, there has been no evidence of powdered ricin brought into the village. Neither does anyone produce nor make ricin here too. So how can there be deaths because of ricin poisoning?" Surya was high on suspense and Rahul was not coming to the point. This angered Surya and he said, "I don't know, Rahul. And I will not know until you bloody tell me." This brought Rahul to the present moment as he was lost in his thoughts questioning himself about the weird twist the case had taken. Rahul realized this and said, "The poison found in the teacup is Jimson weed."

"Jimson weed? What is it?"

"I don't know. Apparently, the tea was made by boiling leaves of Jimson weed. At least that's the poison found in the teacup which your mother drank." These words reminded Surya of his mother's death. For a minute he had been so involved in the technical aspects of the case that he had forgotten that the victim this time was his own mother. He thought '*I have seen my share of deaths as a policeman but nothing quite prepares you for the death of your loved ones.*' Rahul then broke his chain of thought. He had been surfing the web about Jimson weed and later said looking at his phone, "It says here, Jimson weed is a plant which produces poisonous seeds and leaves. It is commonly found along old fields and wastelands and is also cultivated by some for medicinal purposes. And the important part here is that it is found and cultivated in India including Karnataka and Andhra too." Rahul then put down his phone and continued, "I think we got our weapon of crime." Surya listened to Rahul patiently and then asked Rahul, "So do you think all the murders have taken place by Jimson weed? How is it even possible?"

"I'm not saying for sure, but maybe, yeah. It's something we can't rule out."

"So are you saying all the forensics reports are false?"

"Listen, Surya, I'm not implying anything with surety."

Surya interrupted him by saying, "Then? What do you mean?" Rahul knew there was no point in arguing anything without concrete evidence and hence he said, "There's only one way we find out if the forensics are true. I think you need to call up the presiding officer, who has taken charge of this case and ask him about the forensics on your mother's body. The answer may give us some sense of clarity." Surya thought for a moment and then decided that this was the only way they could know for sure. Hence he reached out to his left side where his phone was kept on the table and dialled a number. He was calling his subordinate's phone for the information as he did not know who was the presiding officer on the case after his absence. After some rings, he heard a friendly voice on his phone, "Sir. Good afternoon, sir." It was Chandan Raj, one of Surya's most trusted men on the force. Surya answered, "Yeah, good afternoon… Good afternoon."

"Sir, I can't tell you how glad I'm to hear your voice. I hope you are alright now, sir. I had come to visit you yesterday but you were still in critical care."

"Oh, is it? For now, I'm out of critical care and in the general ward."

"That's great to hear sir." There was then a brief moment of silence and then Chandan continued, "I'm very sorry to hear about your mother's death, sir. I can't imagine what you are going through." Surya closed his eyes for a moment as if to swallow his sadness. Then he began to speak, "Listen, I called you regarding work. I want you to call me immediately when the forensics report on my mother's body comes. This is a matter of urgency and I want you to be discreet. No one should know that I asked you this."

Chandan then spoke, "Sir, the reports have already come."

"What? When?" Surya was surprised that the reports had come this early. He had never heard of or seen police bureaucracy working this quickly. Then he thought that it might be because of the media attention this case was getting. Chandan answered, "Yes. It came today morning, sir."

"And what is the cause of death?" asked Surya.

"Poisoning by ricin, sir. It looks like the work of the same killer who killed other people in the village and who tried to kill you too."

"Are you sure?" asked Surya.

"Yes sir. 100 percent sure."

"Ok thanks, Chandan. Remember to keep this conversation discreet," and he disconnected the call.

"So what is it?" asked a curious Rahul.

Surya then replied, "It's ricin poisoning." This brought a glitter to Rahul's eyes which were meaning to say *I told you so*. He then spoke, "You know what this means? Right?"

Surya replied, "Yes. So this means the forensics is compromised. Am I right?" "Yes. And if this happens to be the case, we can't trust any of the forensics reports we got till now. Maybe all these murders that have taken place including the attempt on your life and your mother's suicide were by Jimson weed poisoning."

"But why is the killer targeting only people who have been sexually abused as a child by this boilersuit person? And why would my mother commit suicide?" asked a frustrated Surya looking for some clarity.

"The only way we can find these answers is by investigating. You need to recover quickly so we can get back on the case." Rahul then continued, "Let me get the doctor to ask him how much more time will it take until they discharge you." After saying this he got up to go see the doctor. While walking he was still surfing on the phone about Jimson weed. As he got to the door of Surya's ward all of a sudden, he stopped and said, "OH SHIT!!" This startled Surya who asked, "What happened?" to which Rahul replied, "The scientific name for Jimson weed is Datura and it is the Sanskrit word for Jimson weed too."

Surya then asked vaguely, "So what if the scientific and Sanskrit word for Jimson weed is Datura? What difference does it make?" Rahul had heard this word before, and chants of *JAI DATURA…JAI DATURA!!!* echoed through his mind.

19

2014, Rampura, Karnataka

Surya just parked his motorcycle in the garage of Kavita's home. The garage already had four cars parked in it and Surya had to fit his bike between two cars to get space for his bike. The motorcycle was one of the few assets his father had left behind after his demise. Surya's father was an honest cop who never indulged in bribery and took a great amount of pride in it. After his demise, his family had to spend every penny with caution. Most of his family's savings would be needed for Surya's higher education and Surya knew it well. This was the reason why Surya was now at Kavita's residence. He had volunteered to help with Tanusha's homeschooling by tutoring her in history and political science for a modest fee. He could always use the extra money.

Kavita was very possessive regarding her daughter. She did not want another one of her children to flee the village for education and a career. Hence she never gave Tanusha the experience of education with other students her age. After finishing her primary education Tanusha was home-schooled for the rest. Kavita did not want her daughter to get ideas of moving to the city for better education and career and she made sure of that. First by giving her the best standard of correspondence education and secondly by always keeping her close to herself and providing her with all the love she could shower on her so that Tanusha would feel guilty about leaving her mother.

Surya passed by the servants and the gardener whom he acknowledged by a wave of his hand. Later he knocked on the main door which was answered by Kavita herself. Kavita smiled at Surya and indicated that Tanusha was up in her room waiting for him. Surya climbed the stairs and knocked on the door of Tanusha's room which was immediately opened by Tanusha. She was glad to see him and her eyes had the sparkle like she was waiting for him.

It had been six months now since Surya had been tutoring Tanusha. Both of them gelled instantly. Surya was a good teacher and more than that was a charming young man. This attracted Tanusha. She had been tutored by slightly elder teachers all her life and the young, handsome and charming personality that was Surya's was a pleasant and welcome change. Over the days that had passed by Surya and Tanusha had become the best of friends. Not a day would pass by without the two of them talking or texting each other. Surya was left all alone after Rahul moved out of the village and had very few people whom he could call genuine friends. Tanusha was one of them if not the closest.

Tanusha sat down at her table and Surya on his seat. Tanusha then asked, "Why didn't you pick up my call last night?" to which Surya replied, "I was tired last night and dozed off early. Why? Were there any doubts on the test I gave you on European Renaissance?"

"Oh, no. I finished my test early evening. Have no doubts."

"Then why did you call?"

"I just felt like it. Why, shouldn't I?"

Surya smiled and replied with sarcasm, "Well my royal lady, I don't think you need to call me unless you have any doubts regarding what I teach you. So better spend less time on your phone and more with your books." Tanusha squeezed her face with an annoying expression, "My God, you are such a dork," after which Surya chuckled. Tanusha continued, "Or I think you have some girlfriend you have not told me about."

"You know that's not true. I'm so shy around girls."

Tanusha replied, "Well you are not shy around me"

"Oh sorry, I meant pretty girls," said Surya. Tanusha became annoyed by this and threw the first thing she saw on her desk at Surya. Surya caught the thing she threw with great agility. He then had a look at the thing she chucked at him and it happened to be her personal journal. He then said, "Well… Well…Well…look at what we have here. It's someone's journal." This immediately alarmed Tanusha as she did not want him to read her journal as she thought it would be embarrassing. She pounced out of her chair and tried to snatch away the journal from Surya. But Surya was adamant about reading it and hence made efforts to shield it from her. He got out of his seat and started running around the room to which Tanusha chased him around. He was way too quick for her. She realized this and pushed him to the wall so he could not have any escape. Then she moved towards the wall but Surya was still adamant about not giving her the journal at any cost until he read it. Tanusha then said, "Surya, you better give me the book."

Surya replied, "Or what?"

"I don't think you want to know."

"I'm reading it at any cost."

"No, you are not."

"You can't stop me."

"I can," as she finished saying this she leaned forward and kissed Surya. This took Surya by surprise. He looked at her. The playful mood no longer existed. Their eyes met and then Surya put his palm on her face and kissed her back. This time it lasted longer with both of them passionately at it with their eyes closed. Then Surya immediately pulled back after a while coming back to reality. He looked regretful. Tanusha saw the expression on his face and asked with great worry, "Was that not good?"

Surya replied, "No... NO... No... It was. It really was. It's just that... uh... I think... I think I need to leave." Surya grabbed his bag from the table and took his keys and stormed out of the room. He came outside the house and pulled his bike out of the garage. He now realized that he was attracted to Tanusha for sure. But he knew nothing between them was ever going to work out in the long run. This was because of the class divide that existed between them. He also felt that it would be breaking Kavita's trust if he was to go forward with anything. So he thought it would be better to end this off right there before it went forward. Before he started his motorcycle, he had one last look up at the window of Tanusha's room. She wasn't to be seen. She was seated on her bed with tears in her eyes as she did not expect it to go the way she imagined it would. She really liked Surya and hence the reaction was not one she liked. Surya started his motorcycle and rode out through the gate onto the road. This was the last time Surya would ever come to tutor her. He later focused on his own career and hence moved to Mangalore for his higher education and police training.

Surya's and Tanusha's romantic flicker was one that ignited and extinguished too quickly, though they would argue if it ever was a romantic flicker.

20

2020, Rampura, Karnataka

"Rahul, you need to tell me. Where have you heard this Datura word before?" asked Surya who was curious to know what Rahul knew. Rahul was lost in his thoughts before answering, "Surya, you have a lot on your plate right now. This day has already been taxing enough for you. You need to rest. Once you recover after a couple of days, I'll explain everything to you."

"Rahul, NO! You need to tell me now. There are people's lives at stake. Who knows how many more people might get killed by this psycho."

"You need to rest. It's not like you can do much right now. For now, I've got a lead. I'll follow that and see what comes to light"

"But…," he was interrupted by Rahul who assured him, "Just a couple of more days, Surya. For now, just focus on recovering rapidly." After saying this Rahul turned and walked out through the door of the ward. Surya was livid with his situation as he couldn't do anything right then. This made him frustrated.

After he took a couple of minutes to calm down, a strike of realization hit him again that his mother was no more.

He couldn't believe what had transpired over the last few days when he was in critical care. His physical pain no more mattered to him in front of the deep sorrow that lay in his heart. His eyes became filled. As he closed his eyes trickles of tears flowed down his cheek. He wiped them with his hand. Surya was a person who seldom cried. All the moments he had with his mother, sweet and sour flashed before him as he closed his eyes.

He spent the next couple of minutes recollecting these memories until his chain of thinking was broken by a knock on his door. He wondered who it might be. He only wished for the one person he wanted to see on the other side of the door, which was his mother. But as the door opened it was Tanusha. The only other woman in his life who was special to him. She smiled as she entered which was like a remedy that salved his wounds. She then came and sat on the chair beside him. Tanusha then said, "Surya, I'm sorry to hear about your mother." These words filled his eyes again. Tanusha then continued, "I came all these days to visit you but you were not doing well. I can't imagine the pain you are going through right now." Surya didn't utter a word. She then continued again, "I hear you are recovering well now and will be out in a matter of days. That's relieving to hear." Surya still lay silent just looking at her. Tanusha was put off by him not replying and then said, "I'm sorry Surya. Should I have not come?" Surya then realized his silence and then said, "No. It's just that I'm happy to see you. I can't be more glad that you are here." This brought a smile to Tanusha's face which in turn brought a smile on Surya's too. Surya then asked, "Tanusha, did you speak to my mother, before you know…she did what she did?"

"No. We are all shocked by this incident. Just heard what Rahul had to say. Sharda aunty would never do such a thing. Not as far as we know."

"When did you last see her?"

"Uh, I think the evening before she passed away. She had been with us to Guruji's gathering"

"And did anything seem off about her?"

"No. She was behaving exactly as usual with us. We couldn't make out anything different with her. I really can't believe she killed herself."

Surya then put his hand on his face and took a deep breath. Then continued to say, "I should have been with her that night. I was so fucking consumed with work that I couldn't look after my own mother. I couldn't recognize her suffering."

"No, Surya, no. You can't blame yourself for this." She held his hand and then continued, "You couldn't possibly know. None of us could make out her suffering."

Surya was frustrated with himself now. He said, "But I'm her son. I'm the only one she had after dad passed away. It was my responsibility to look after her, and I've failed miserably." Surya again broke into tears and started weeping. This made Tanusha shed tears too. She then got up and embraced Surya. He clasped her back too. It was like both of them had deep wounds in their hearts which were cured instantly by holding each other. She then moved back still holding Surya. Now they could feel each other's breaths. A feeling of warmth emerged between them. Then Tanusha moved even closer and their lips met as they kissed. They kissed for a moment or two before Surya pulled back. This made Tanusha awkward and she said, "Uh, I think I should leave."

Surya then instantly said, "No… uh, I mean, don't."

"Why? Do you want me to stay?"

Surya then held her face gently and kissed her back passionately. This time it lasted for a while longer. Then Surya pulled back and while still holding her face said to her, "Yes, I want you to stay." This brought a smile to Tanusha's face again which in turn made Surya smile. He then wondered, *how did her one smile have the power to heal all his wounds?*

21

2020, Rampura, Karnataka

The environment in Guruji Vishwas's Ashram was calming. Rahul sat in the rear end of the hall with a book. He had been reading the guide and information book on Guruji Vishwas and his teachings. At the front end of the hall, there was a group of 25 people who were guided in meditation by an instructor. Rahul noticed that the instructor was a young male who might still be in his early twenties. This surprised Rahul. He always thought to be a teacher of meditation you needed to have experience and hence would be more of an elder person. But then again this was no ordinary religious gathering. At least that seemed to be the case from the information Rahul got from reading the book.

From his readings, Rahul realized that this was actually not a religious gathering as it welcomed people of all religions to be their followers. Unlike other religious gatherings, it did not seek to convert people of their religions. People from all religions were welcome. In fact, the teachings of Guruji actually promoted their followers to continue to keep their own faith of choice or birth. This gathering was meant to be a healing process for people with suffering who couldn't find solace or peace through any other method.

Also in the book, the life of Guruji Vishwas was described. Guruji Vishwas was an orphan. He was abandoned as a baby by his parents near a cave in Uttarakhand where Rishis used to meditate. The cave was called Vashishta Cave. According to Hindu mythology, the Vashishta Cave was where the great sage Vashishta meditated. This was a hotspot where Rishis and Yogis came to meditate to reach enlightenment. Vishwas was picked up by the local Rishis and was brought up by them. He was taught the art of meditation which he grew fond of. He practised deep meditation for many years and eventually claimed to be enlightened. However, Vishwas didn't associate his meditation and enlightenment with any particular religion. Hence he left the place and started preaching his own teachings to people throughout the country. After some years he gained quite some following. And now he was stationed in Karnataka for a few months to preach, where he wanted to build his own permanent Ashram.

Rahul was quite impressed with Guruji's journey. He then closed the book and walked to the reception of the Ashram where he returned the book he had borrowed. At the reception were a lady and a short man in Ashram's outfit. He wanted to inquire about something at the reception. Details of everything regarding the Ashram were present in the book except that of Jimson weed or the so-called *Datura*. This was the reason he had come to the Ashram. So Rahul said to the receptionist lady, "Good afternoon. I wanted to inquire about something." The receptionist lady greeted him with a kind smile and then said, "Yes sir. Sure. How can I help you?"

"I wanted to know more about Datura. Uh, actually I was impressed with Guruji's teachings and wanted to get a plant for myself. What is the process for this?" As soon as Rahul said this, the short man's attention went towards Rahul. Till now the man wasn't interested in what was happening at the reception and was busy working on something. Rahul noticed the sudden attention he got from the man. The receptionist, on the other hand, said with an even kinder smile, "I'm very sorry, sir, but the Datura is cared for by Guruji himself. You can come here for Darshan of the Datura and meditate with it, but it's not for sale."

Rahul then said, "Oh, is it?"

The receptionist then replied, "Yes sir. But the policies are changing on December 15th. You may come then and inquire about the same."

"Why? What's special about December 15th?"

"It's the date Guruji gained enlightenment for the first time."

"Oh, is it? Wonderful!"

"Where are you from, sir?"

"I'm from Bangalore. My name is Rahul. I'm part of the press. I came here to report on the ricin poisoning murders." As soon as Rahul said this the man started to look a bit worried. Rahul could sense the tension in this man. This man began to perspire. However, the receptionist on the other hand looked calm as ever and said, "Oh, ok. It's a sad thing that happened here, sir. I hope the police find answers soon."

Rahul then said, "Yes, we are all hoping for the same." But Rahul was still observing this man as he continued to perspire. Then after a moment the man took his phone out and left the reception area to a back door while texting on his phone. A moment after the man left, Rahul asked the receptionist lady, "Who is that man?"

"Who? Sathish? He is a part of our crew. He handles and manages the nursery where we grow our Datura plants." Finally, Rahul got a lead he could follow. Something seemed off-putting about this man to Rahul. And now he knew what this man did. Rahul then thanked the receptionist for her kind conversation and left the Ashram. He knew what to do next.

22

Two Days Later, Rampura, Karnataka

Rahul and Surya sat in the Maruti Swift, closely keeping an eye on the chemist shop that lay ahead of them. At the front of the chemist shop stood Sathish, who constantly kept looking at his watch which indicated that he was waiting for someone. Rahul had followed Sathish to the same chemist shop two days back. Sathish looked frustrated that day before he went into the chemist shop and came out after 10 minutes. From there Rahul followed him straight back to the Ashram. However, this time he had brought Surya along. Just this morning Surya had been discharged from the hospital and he was already back on the job. Though he was not allowed to join the case officially for investigation because of his health, he decided to conduct his own investigation alongside Rahul. Surya knew he was not in the prime of health but his conscience had not allowed him to rest until the perpetrator was caught.

Rahul had brought Surya up-to-date on the case. Surya was shocked to learn that the Ashram may probably be involved in these murders. So there the two of them waited in stealth in their car as Sathish waited for someone else to open the chemist shop. After waiting for around half an hour Sathish's phone beeped indicating that he had got a message. Sathish grabbed his phone from his pocket and had a look. Immediately he became tensed and started looking around until he spotted the Swift car Rahul and Surya were in. They had done a good job hiding from plain sight until then, but Sathish had now spotted them. Rahul and Surya realized this and Rahul started his car in anticipation that Sathish would try to escape. Sathish immediately started walking in the opposite direction of the car. Surya said to Rahul, "Take the car to him." Rahul put his foot on the gas lightly and started driving towards Sathish. As Rahul approached Sathish, Surya said to him, "Sathish, get in the car." Sathish recognized Rahul from earlier in the day and also recognized Surya as the police officer. But Sathish replied in the negative saying, "Why should I? I haven't done anything wrong. And why are you following me?"

Surya said again, "Sathish, it would be better if you get inside. We just have a few things we need to discuss. That's all."

"No. I don't have anything I want to discuss with any of you. In turn, it would be better if you guys stopped following me."

Surya knew that it wasn't going to be easy to get him inside the car. So he pulled out his gun which he had brought with him. Rahul was shocked to see the gun and quite frankly frightened. "What are you doing?" asked a frightened Rahul. Surya replied, "Wait. I've got this. You want him inside the car. This is how it's going to happen." So he pointed the gun at Sathish and asked him once again, "Better get inside. We just want to talk." Sathish now got frightened and immediately took off running in the other direction. Surya immediately got out of the car and started running behind Sathish. Now it was a chase. Sathish picked up the pace and took a sharp turn inside a gully. Following him, Surya also took a turn. Now both were at their maximum pace running through the small, narrow gullies. However, Surya struggled to keep up with Sathish due to his ill health but was trying his best. It was quiet in the village as it was midnight and everyone was fast asleep. Sathish ran from one gully to another being followed and chased by Surya. However, after some time Surya felt his stomach churning and knew that he could not keep running for long. So he stopped and raised his gun aiming at Sathish's leg. He was about to pull the trigger when he was struck by a thought. He realized that it was midnight and firing his gun would bring unnecessary attention. So he put the gun behind his back and again started chasing Sathish. But now Sathish had gone far off. It would be impossible for Surya to chase and catch him. So Surya gave up the chase. But to his luck, Rahul had reached the other side of the road and struck Sathish with his car. This blow made Sathish fall down in front of the car. Rahul got out of the car immediately and held Sathish who was now growling in pain after the crash. Soon Surya came and held Sathish by his collar and got him inside the car in the backseat. He took Sathish's phone from his pocket and read the message he had received. The message was from an unsaved private number. After reading the message he showed it to Rahul. It read, 'Someone is following you. Can't meet now. Move from there.' Rahul and Surya looked at each other and then got inside the car. Surya sat in the backseat gripping Sathish while Rahul drove from there.

23

2020, Rampura, Karnataka

It was half past two in the wee hours of the morning. Sathish was forcefully seated on the chair with hands and legs tied up and a tape to his mouth. They had got him inside Rahul's guesthouse with Surya holding a gun to Sathish's gut warning him not to call for help as it would lead to dire consequences. Surya didn't want to grab unnecessary attention because he knew well, that he was operating outside the law. Rahul on the other hand was in panic mode as soon as Surya wielded the gun in his car.

Surya removed the tape from Sathish's mouth. "You scream or call for help, I will not hesitate to use the gun on you," said Surya, "Understood?" Sathish wasn't ready to be caught that day. He knew well that he would be in some kind of trouble one day or another but never expected it to be this soon. Sathish was a man from Mangalore who had followed Guruji for some time now. He was impressed with Guruji's teachings and joined his entourage when Guruji visited Mangalore. However, he was a man with greed for money and always used to conduct some side business in Guruji's organization wherever they went to make some extra fortunes. This was done without the knowledge of Guruji and the organization.

"You know, I'll make sure you get in deep trouble for this. I very well know you are no longer on this case. So let me go and I spare your career," said Sathish to Surya. Surya on hearing this felt a jolt of anger run through his body and punched Sathish in his face. The blow was quite hard as Sathish started to bleed from his mouth. Then Surya said, "You talk in this tone to me and you won't be in any position to make sure anything ever." Sathish laughed at Surya on hearing him exuberating this strange sense of confidence. "The whole system is working with me. What can you do after all?"

"I guessed that. We know that ricin wasn't used in the poisoning and it was Jimson weed, or should I call Datura."

"So?"

"So you better start speaking. Why did you kill these people in the village?" Surya spoke as he showed the pictures of the victims to Sathish.

"I didn't kill any of them," Sathish said vaguely. Surya landed another blow on Sathish's nose which made him bleed from the nose this time. Then he asked again, "Why did you kill these people? You better answer this time or it's going to get a lot worse for you." Rahul sat in the corner of the room closing his eyes now and then to avoid looking at the violence unfolding before his eyes. Then Sathish spoke again, "I didn't kill any of them. How much ever you're going to hit me my answer will be the same."

"No, no, no, no, no. I ain't going to hit you again." Saying this Surya moved to the other side of the room and came back with a plier. This frightened Sathish a bit wondering what Surya might do next. Rahul got up and tried to stop Surya, "Hey hey hey… what are you doing?"

"I'm doing what's necessary. The same thing you would also do if you wanted answers for your mother's death." Saying this Surya moved closer to Sathish. He asked again, "Why did my mother kill herself?"

"Your mother? What? How will I know?" answered a rather clueless Sathish. Surya after hearing this reply immediately bent down, held Sathish's right foot and using the plier removed the whole nail off Sathish's thumb. After this, he immediately held Sathish's mouth not allowing him to scream. Sathish cried out in pain not being able to scream. Rahul could not bear to see this and almost puked. Then Surya asked, "I'm asking you again. Why did you kill them?" Sathish crying out said, "I did not." Surya bent down and held Sathish's foot again. He almost pulled another nail out with the pliers but before he could do this Sathish said, "Ok, ok… I'll tell you." Surya stopped and Rahul was as much relieved as Sathish.

"Speak."

"I did poison the victims. But I received money for it. Did it on someone's orders"

"On whose orders?"

"I don't know."

"What do you mean?"

"The person always came in a boilersuit with an animal mask of different animals each time." Rahul and Surya looked at each other with shock. Then Sathish continued, "The person never talked to me and always wrote the name of the victim to be killed with the address on a sheet of paper and gave it to me. I received the money from the person on spot."

Then Surya asked, "Did the person always meet you at the chemist shop?"

"Yes. I met the person inside the chemist shop."

"And today also you came to meet him?"

"Yes." Then Surya came near Rahul and said, "I need to make a call to find out in whose name that abandoned chemist shop is registered. As he was meeting the perpetrator inside the shop, the boiler suit person must be the owner of the shop. Also, I asked about the number through which the message was sent. It was traced back to a man from Mysore named Ramanna. It so happens that Ramanna died early this year and his phone is being used illegally by someone else whom we have no idea about. But the most interesting part is that Ramanna was one of the founding trustees of Gurujis Ashram and he had no family that we know of apart from the people he knew and met at the Ashram. The phone number is being tracked right now and the location is showing somewhere near the outskirts of the village. So there we have some hope." He said this and moved to another side of the room to make the phone call. He dialled Chandan Raj.

Rahul, on the other hand, moved over to the window to look outside. He wanted to know if anyone had caught the air of what they were doing. He was especially worried about the owners of the guest house as they lived just beneath his room. But after looking he was reassured that no one knew what was going on inside his room. He was still looking out the window when a hand touched his shoulder. It took him by surprise as he was intently focusing elsewhere. He moved and turned in shock. But it was just Surya who later said, "The chemist shop is registered to MLA Sanjay Khadke."

"What?"

"And the phone we were tracking was tied to a street dog around its collar and we were tracking nothing but the movements of the dog."

2020, Rampura, Karnataka

Rahul looked around him as his sight was filled with various photos of MLA Sanjay Khadke with the top state leadership dignitaries of the current administration. This also included a photo of him standing right beside the Chief Minister of Karnataka where he was seen welcoming by a garland of flowers the CM who was donning with great pride his kurta of the saffron cloth which had become the winning symbol of the party. Rahul was one who never cared much about politics during his university days but his job slowly required him to be well-versed in the political theatre of the nation which he was successful at.

Surya, on the other hand, was sitting right beside Rahul on a sofa that had an antique quality to it. This was not the first time he had been to MLA Sanjay Khadke's house. He had visited previously to provide and arrange protection for the MLA whenever the leader took out his controversial processions and protests. But this time it was different as it was for another matter altogether. After Sathish's confession, Surya and Rahul had long contemplated and discussed over the night and had come to the decision to visit Sanjay Khadke's house as soon as the sun was up and maybe even call him for questioning over the identity of the suspected man in the boilersuit. They thought if anyone would know a hint about the man in the boilersuit it would be the MLA as he owned the chemist shop. They had also dared to think that the MLA might be the man in the boilersuit as Surya had been trained never to rule out any angle when it came to serial murders and killers. It could be the most unexpected person behind it all. After all, the truth was stranger than fiction when it came to crime.

Rahul and Surya were almost tired of waiting for the MLA and were about to inquire if the MLA was even ready to meet them when he finally appeared from upstairs wearing a white kurta and pyjamas. He was a tall man with a rather fit personality for someone of his age. As soon as he got down he came close to Surya and shook his hand. He then said, "I heard about your poisoning. I hope you are well now."

"Yes, sir. It's been a tough week," replied Surya.

"I'm sorry to hear about your mother too. Family is everything and I can't imagine your pain. My deepest condolences." Surya nodded his head. Rahul could already understand the reason behind the growth of this politician from rags to riches when he witnessed his charm first-hand. Rahul also witnessed the humility of the leader though he could not confirm if it was genuine or a facade as was the case with many of his counterparts and colleagues in this field of work. The MLA then finally acknowledged Rahul with a nod of his head and a smile and indicated for them to be seated. He also took his seat on the main sofa. He then asked, "So, tell me. To what do I owe this visit?"

"We wanted to inquire about the closed chemist shop that you own," said Surya.

The MLA thought for a while trying to remember which shop they were talking about and after a couple of moments, it struck him. He then asked, "Why?"

"We believe it has something to do with the serial murders that have taken place in the village."

"That shop? How?" he was puzzled.

"Before answering that question, we would like to know for how long you have owned that chemist shop."

"It's been a long time since I have owned it."

"For how long exactly?"

The MLA took a short pause, then said, "I'm confused. I thought you were no longer investigating the case."

"Officially I'm not. But circumstances are such that I chose to continue with my investigation and the police force could always use the extra help," replied Surya.

"Hmm, I see. But if you ask me, I think you should take some time to grieve. It's an irreparable loss that you have incurred this past week. Work can always take a back seat when it comes to these matters."

"I think I'll do just fine, Mr. Khadke. But I appreciate the concern. Now, can we please get to the matter at hand? Lots of lives may still be at stake here."

"Hmm. What is it exactly that you associate with that long-closed shop?"

Surya for a second or two calculated all the risks of letting the man know about the investigation and then finally said, "We believe that the main accused must have been using the place as a decoy point or a safe house." The politician chuckled. But when he realized that Surya wasn't joking, he said, "That's not possible. As you already mentioned, the place has been shut for years."

Surya contemplated, then said, "Well, we have strong evidence to back this information."

"What evidence is that?"

"You know I can't tell you that."

"Then who is the accused?"

Surya now was getting his patience tested by the man with all his counter questions. But he swallowed the feeling and said, "The accused? Well, you tell me. That's what we are here for."

The politician gave a stern expression and asked, "How would I know?"

Rahul who was silent all along interrupted and said, "Well it's your shop. And it has been for a long time now. You should be aware of the happenings on your property." The politician was taken aback by this unknown person making a statement about him. After all, in spite of being a humble person he was not used to being talked to like that. At least for some years now. So he said, "I don't know you. So please introduce yourself." Surya now sensed that the man was not impressed by the tone Rahul spoke. So he said, "This is one of my associates. We go long back. So anything you can tell me, you can tell him."

The MLA stared at Rahul for a while as if trying to judge whether he was a safe person. Surya noticed this and finally decided to say, "Ok. Let me get straight to the point. The main suspect for these murders has also been involved in a series of pedophilia cases from many years ago. He always preys on his victims wearing a boilersuit with an animal mask. So do you have any idea who it is?" "What?" asked Mr. Khadke and then started to laugh which both Surya and Rahul found annoying. He then realized that they were serious and then asked, "Who do you think is that man?"

Surya said, "We were hoping you would know."

The MLA understood what they meant, "Listen, if you are making an assumption that I may be involved somehow, you can't be more wrong and I find this very insulting and vicious on your part."

Rahul now said, "If not you, it can be one of your associates too. As I said, it's your property and you should be knowing well."

Now the politician started to fume, "Listen. I'm a businessman along with being a politician. I have numerous properties that I buy and sell regularly. That's how I make my fortune. I'm an honest politician who works for the people and hence need to make my money somewhere else to survive in this field of politics. The chemist shop is one such property that I have bought and have left unused. Sure, I may have access to the shop but I can assure you none of my family, followers, or I have anything to do with these crimes. The time you spend here you could be spending at the right place to catch the criminal."

Surya took a long pause staring at the MLA right in his eyes as if trying to judge the authenticity of the words he just heard. He then broke the silence and asked, "Who did you buy it from? Maybe the former owner may still have the keys to the chemist shop and access to the property."

Sanjay Khadke took a short pause thinking, before saying, "I bought the land and the shop that stands on it from a woman named Kavita. She belongs to an influential family in this village." Surya was shocked to hear this and immediately looked at Rahul who was still looking at the politician with great shock himself and exclaimed, "WHAT?"

25

2020, Rampura, Karnataka

Mr. Sanjay Khadke opened the lock on the main door of the chemist shop. It opened rather with great smoothness and swift motion. He was taken aback by surprise. Rahul who was standing right beside him asked, "Why do you look surprised?"

"For a building that hasn't been used in years, I am surprised that the locks still function so smoothly. I expected it to be a bit more rustic by now." Rahul was satisfied with the answer. He had accompanied the MLA to investigate and have a look at the abandoned chemist shop while Surya, on the other hand, had gone back to Rahul's guest house to hand over Sathish to the cops. Rahul and Surya had left Sathish who was unconscious now by the beating he took tied to a chair in the guest house and had locked all the doors and windows from the outside.

Rahul entered the chemist shop after the MLA. As soon as they entered, Rahul had a look at the abandoned shop. His immediate reaction was that it looked as abandoned from the inside as was the building from the outside. It was a medium-sized shop. The floors were dusty which indicated that they hadn't been cleaned in years. There were no medicines left in the shop apart from a first-aid kit lying around and a few bottles of coloured liquids on the shelves which Rahul assumed were syrups left around. As Rahul started to have a look around the shop he asked, "When exactly did my mother sell this shop to you?" "Probably it has been a decade," answered the MLA. The MLA too looked around the shop as if it was a strange place to him. By his reactions, you could not tell that he was the owner of this shop. This showed how rarely he visited the building.

After looking around for a while Rahul did not find anything strange about the shop. It looked just like an abandoned pharmacy. So he thought of returning and going outside when suddenly the MLA shouted out Rahul's name from the back end of the shop. Rahul walked swiftly to the back end and discovered that the MLA had found a small door. He opened the door to discover a cabin lying behind it. It was dark and Rahul moved his hands around the wall of the cabin hoping to find the switch to the lights. Finally, he found the switch and turned on the lights. As soon as the lights were on, he discovered a rather clean and tidy cabin. It looked like someone had maintained it for a while now and was totally opposite from the rest of the shop. Before he could acknowledge it his eyes lay on the other side of the wall where he found a variety of boiler suits of various colours hanging on it. And besides the suits lay hanging a variety of animal masks. Rahul finally found what he was looking for and before he could realize it, he saw several pots with plants on the floor. He immediately recognized the plants as Jimson weeds. It was as if all his investigation had led him here. Rahul bent down to have a look at the plants. He was careful enough not to touch the leaves. He started examining it closely and suddenly he found something lying on the back of one of the pots. He moved the pot carefully and there he found a book. He got hold of the book. It was dusty so he cleaned the dust off it by removing a kerchief from his pocket. Slowly the title of the book on the cover page became visible. It read 'Teachings and experience of Jonestown'.

Rahul knew what it was he just read. He knew of Jonestown and was well-versed with the happenings there. He got more worried when he found a saffron robe and small strips of black cloth lying under where the book was found. Things started to become clear to him now. He knew that a cult was operating in the village of which his mother and sister were a part and finding this evil book worried him more. He started to see parallels between both. "We need to inform this to Surya," said Rahul to the MLA. Both of them came out of the cabin and out of the abandoned shop. As soon as they reached outside Rahul took out his phone from his pocket to call Surya. Before he could dial Surya, a car came out from the road and parked in front of the shop. Rahul recognized the car though it took him a moment in the rush of things. A man drenched in blood all over his shirt and trousers got out of the driver's seat. Rahul was shocked to see the man. It was none other than Surya.

26

2020, Rampura, Karnataka

Rahul immediately moved towards Surya and asked him, "What the hell happened? Why are you all covered in blood?" MLA Sanjay Khadke was also taken aback by the sight of Surya being drenched in blood. Without answering Rahul, Surya walked over to Sanjay furiously with great rage and held him by the collar, and asked, "What did you do? Who did you send? Tell me why I shouldn't kill you right here right now." The MLA looked at him confused and asked, "What do you mean? What did I do?"

"You know well what you did."

"NO! For God's sake will you take your hand off my collar?"

"I'll fucking kill you right now, motherfucker!"

"What are you talking about? Do you know who you are talking to? If you want to live you better take your hands off my collar."

"What if I don't, huh? You going to kill me too?"

Rahul now interrupted them and asked, "Surya, what are you doing? Let him go." Surya replied to Rahul, "Why should I? He just had Sathish killed."

"WHAT!" exclaimed Rahul. Khadke was shocked by this revelation too. "I did not have anyone killed. What are you talking about?" Rahul now was eternally dazed and confused to a point where he required some immediate answers. So he went forward to Surya and asked, "What happened? You need to tell me what happened there?"

"I went to the guest house to hand over Sathish to the police, but when I reached there Sathish was lying on the floor with the chair to his back and a pool of blood lying beside him. Someone had broken the lock to your room and had entered. Then I moved closer to Sathish and that is when I realized that someone had shot him in the chest three times. I think I reached there just a few minutes after the person who shot him left the room. I still felt the pulse in him and tried to save him. I immediately called for an ambulance and then tried to ask Sathish about the person who did this. But he wasn't in a state to reply and succumbed to the bullet shots before the ambulance reached there."

"How do you know Sanjay did it?" asked Rahul. "He was here with me the entire time."

"Of course, he didn't pull the trigger himself. He had one of his men do the dirty work for him."

The MLA now spoke, "I didn't do it nor did I send any of my men to do it. Why would I even think of doing it?"

"Because you are the one who ordered the killings that Sathish carried out and now wanted to cover your tracks," said Surya.

"How can you say that?" asked Rahul.

"Rahul, it makes sense. Who else knew about where we held Sathish? Apart from you, me, and Ramesh, it was Khadke who knew about Sathish and the place we held him." Rahul now pondered about that thought. Khadke on the other hand shouted, "I didn't do it. You guys need to believe me. I swear I didn't order the hit on Sathish." Rahul now after much pondering said to Surya, "Surya, I don't think it is that simple. I really don't think it is Sanjay who did this."

"Why are you taking his side?" asked Surya.

"Because I believe that there is something bigger at play here. I just found out about a book and if the cult in this village has anything to do with that book there might be grave consequences at play here. I think we need to interrogate my mother and before that happens I think we should get a hold of this so-called Guruji Vishwas and ask him a few questions." The MLA now spoke, "You can't. Guruji just left the village today. Today is Datura *diwas*. It is something Guruji and all his followers celebrate." Rahul now asked, "What do you mean? Celebrate how?"

"I have no idea. When I sold the land to Guruji he always used to mention this day and would call it a celebration to come." Rahul now was even more worried after what he had heard from the MLA. He spoke, "Surya, we need to interrogate my mother now immediately regarding the ownership of the chemist shop and seeing that she is a follower of Guruji she may have some answers to my questions on Guruji too."

"What is it you are talking about a book? What book do you mean?" asked Surya.

"I'll tell you on the way. For now, we need to get to my mother's place as soon as possible. Sanjay, I think you need to accompany us."

27

2020, Rampura, Karnataka

There was an eerie silence in the car as Rahul, Surya, and Sanjay Khadke headed towards Kavita's bungalow. It had taken some convincing for Surya to settle down his anger after the whole incident with Sathish. Though Rahul had succeeded in calming Surya down, Surya was still a bit sceptical about Khadke. He strongly believed Khadke to be the architect of all that had taken place in the village. But one thing that calmed him was that Khadke was in his sight and it was still not late to apprehend him if Rahul's theory failed to be the fact.

On the other hand, Surya had already alerted the police about Sathish's killing and an alert was issued to close the village borders so that the person who shot Sathish could not flee the village.

It was a 20-minute drive from the chemist shop to Kavita's bungalow. It would have taken a lot less time if the roads were well-constructed and spaced. Though a small stretch of the road was a national highway the interior areas still majorly were poorly developed and tarred roads with potholes every 50 metres. This showed the work done by the MLA who was now in power locally for more than 10 years. Despite doing no noticeable work in these years he was re-elected every time with a thumping majority because he belonged to a majority caste in the village and also his money-spending capacity during elections helped him.

Rahul finally broke the silence by asking Khadke, "For how long have you known Guruji?"

"I came to know about him two years ago when he first arrived in the village with his rather small team. I was impressed with his knowledge and charisma instantly. He had by then spent years abroad studying, preaching, and gaining spiritual knowledge. At least that's what he told me. And for the past four years, he has been travelling all over the state of Karnataka imparting his wisdom and spiritual knowledge."

"What about the land you sold to him?"

"Ah! That was sold to a person by the name of Salim. He is an international businessman who funds, promotes, and manages Guruji's foundation."

"Salim? Wow! Looks like Guruji attracts more than the typical Hindu followers."

"Salim is an outstanding man of great virtue."

"What do you mean by that?"

"I mean that he is a man of his word. And not to mention that his payments were always swift and before time." Surya scoffed at this. He thought to himself that it was no wonder this politician found Salim an upstanding person as it was only money that mattered to Khadke. Rahul continued, "What can you tell me about the payment?"

"Nothing much. Just that he offered triple the price of the land for fast-tracking the selling process."

"Woah! Triple the amount? That seems very generous. Didn't it occur to you that it seems strange that someone would offer triple the price just for fast-tracking the process?"

"Not really, I guess," answered Khadke. "He is reputed and to be frank, quite a wealthy businessman. He is the owner of a large export-import business conglomerate situated in Karachi."

"What?" exclaimed Rahul. "You mean he is a Pakistani national?"

"Yes. You can say so."

"Didn't it occur to you that something strange might be at play here while you do business with a Pakistan national?"

"Not really. He seemed to be a staunch follower of Guruji Vishwas and his ideals. He wanted to spend the rest of his life after retirement, promoting Guruji and his foundation."

"Ok, let us say that I'm convinced he is an ardent follower of the cult. But aren't you from the party which opposes anything that has to do with Pakistan and its culture? Heck, you guys win elections by spreading hate and venom towards your fellow neighbours. Don't you practise what you preach?"

Khadke gave a witty smile and then said, "Listen, you are a journalist. You very well know that these are election-winning strategies and nothing more. People understand only the language of hate these days and that is what we propagate. Our party right now is the only party in this nation that can bring about great development and positive change. You can consider the hate as a small collateral damage and sacrifice for this nation to achieve great heights and to become a force to reckon with in the world. Not to mention the price he offered was handsome and it will come in handy for me during the next elections if that's the answer you are looking for from me." Rahul and Surya looked at each other and rolled their eyes. But by the time they could say more they had arrived at the bungalow. After parking the car by the side of the road, the three of them got out of the car and headed towards the gate of the bungalow.

28

2020, Rampura, Karnataka

Rahul rang the bell at the main door of the bungalow. They waited for a minute but to no answer. He pressed the bell again but still to no reply from the other end. This time Surya pressed the bell and waits for some moments, but no answer. So Surya now pushed the door and realized that the door was left unlocked. The door opened with great stealth. Now, this raised an alarm in Surya's head and he immediately went for his gun. He readied his gun from his waist and loaded it. Rahul and Khadke also became alert looking at Surya. The three of them realized that the killer who went after Sathish and was still at loose might be present here. There were high chances of that happening.

Rahul was above to call out to his mother and Surya realized this beforehand and hence kept his palm on Rahul's mouth avoiding and warning him not to call out as it might alert the killer. So now Surya takes the lead with his gun cocked and ready as he moved towards the hall. The other two followed just behind him. All three of them were moving now with great stealth. Rahul was worried for his mother and the rest of his family as they could be in grave danger. Khadke on the other hand was fearful for his own life and to be frank a thought passed through his mind to flee from the scene, away from danger and call the police. However, he did not run and his awareness made him reach out for his phone and dial the police as Surya and Rahul stayed busy moving with stealth looking for Kavita and her family.

When they completely scanned the ground floor which consisted of the hall, kitchen, and dining room, Rahul pointed towards the stairs and whispered softly, "Let's go up." Surya nodded his head in affirmation and slowly started climbing the stairs. As they reached the first floor they headed straight to Tanusha's room. They reached the door and Surya pushed it gently, which opened the door and to his distress, found it a worrying situation. He saw Tanusha lying on the bed with foam around her mouth. He immediately scanned the room and when he found it safe, went towards the bed and realized that she was unconscious. Now came the most anxious and nervous moment of all for Surya. He had to check her pulse to determine whether she was still alive. Rahul too was worried out of his wits and nervous at the same time. Surya put his hand to check her pulse and found it beating. A wave of gratitude towards God was felt by Surya at that moment which could not be expressed. He nodded his head to indicate to Rahul that she was alive.

"We need to get her to the hospital immediately," said Surya but realized that neither he nor Rahul could afford to leave the bungalow at that moment without finding Kavita and her husband. So Rahul took out the keys from his pocket and tossed them over to Khadke. Then Surya lifted Tanusha off the bed and handed her over to Khadke. "Get her to the nearby hospital as soon as possible. Now go." Khadke carried her and went down the stairs.

Rahul along with Surya scanned the first floor completely. Kavita and her husband were nowhere to be seen. So they checked the second floor and the roof but to the same results. Then Rahul remembered that they did not visit Chotu's room which was at the back of the bungalow. He indicated to Surya and Surya led the way to the back of the bungalow with Rahul following him. Surya still with his gun cocked and pointed forward moved towards the door of Chotu's room and gently opened it. There he witnessed Kavita kneeling down before a pot of a plant. Rahul immediately recognized it as Jimson weed. Next to her lay a teacup with a drink in it. It was warm as you could see the vapours over it. Before Rahul could reach his mother, he could not avoid looking at his stepfather who was sitting in his wheelchair a few feet away from Kavita. The whole scene was baffling to Rahul and Surya, and something in their gut told them that all was not well. Rahul immediately went over to his mother. "Mother! What's happening? Do you realize that Tanu is unconscious in the other room?"

"Yes," answered a calm Kavita.

"What do you mean 'yes'? Is she in some danger? Are you in some danger?"

"Nothing has ever been better, son."

"What? What's happening? What do you mean by that?"

Kavita was still calm but this time she just closed her eyes and smiled without providing any answer. Rahul looked at the teacup closely and then asked, "Is that what I think it is? Is it Jimson weed tea?"

Kavita now opened her eyes and said, "Yes. You're right. It is."

Now Surya started to connect the dots and finally asked Kavita, "Did you just poison Tanusha with Jimson weed tea?"

Kavita now answered, "No. Not at all. She did that herself."

"But why?"

"Don't you still understand? It's Datura *diwas*."

Rahul now asked, "So?"

"Now I'm going to drink this tea and join Tanusha for eternal healing and happiness."

"What are you talking about? That's madness. Why would you kill yourself? We are not letting you do that."

"Hmm…You tell me now Surya. You were sexually abused as a child. Do you know who did that to you?"

Surya stood there shocked wondering how on earth she knew about it. He had not shared that horrendous experience with anyone. Not even with his own family. He just stood there without any reply looking at Kavita. She then asked him looking at his silence, "You must be wondering how I know that. Right? You know what, let's just forget about that fact for a second. Tell me something. What would you do to the person who did that to you? Hmm, tell me."

"I'm not going to answer that question. First, you tell me, what are you up to here?" asked Surya.

"What would you do to that person? Huh? What justice is there for a horrendous crime like that?"

"Don't you steer away from the point, Kavita. I'm not going to answer your question."

Kavita persisted in asking the same question. "What justice is there for something which stole your childhood away from you? Tell me."

Surya was now getting mentally disturbed by the question, "I'm not going to tell you."

"Well, you need to tell me."

"NO!"

"You need to."

"I'm not."

Kavita now screamed at Surya, "WHAT WOULD YOU DO?"

Surya now lost all his patience and screamed back with his impulse, "I WOULD SHOOT THE PERSON POINT BLANK WHO DID THAT TO ME."

"Well, let me do that for you," said Kavita as she got up quickly and snatched the gun away from his hand, and shot her crippled husband straight through the head. BOOM...

29

2020, Rampura, Karnataka

Brain matter along with blood splashed on the nearest wall as she pressed the trigger. Guru Dutt's head went back permanently resting there. Splashes of blood got onto Kavita's face and also stained her saffron saree. Rahul was taken by shock and shrieked his throat out. Surya who did not have any time to react and retrieve his gun was also taken by surprise but did not scream thanks to the profession he was in, though some could dispute this as local police rarely had to use their weapon lest someone else use it. "OH MY GOD!!!!!! OH MY GOD!!!!! What did you do?" screamed Rahul.

"What needed to be done," replied Kavita.

"What do you mean? Why did you shoot him?"

"I just did what Surya should have done."

"What? What do you mean? You mean he is the one who sexually assaulted Surya?" asked Rahul who barely recovered from what had happened and tried greatly to put those words together. Surya was now still silent but looking at the person whose brains were just blown out.

"Yes. He is the one. He is the man with the mask and boilersuit," said Kavita.

30

2005, Rampura, Karnataka

A four-year-old Tanusha came into Kavita's room while she was busy ironing her clothes. She ran towards her teddy bear and tried to grab it which was in the cabin next to the ironing table.

"Tanu, no. How many times have I told you not to play near the ironing table?" said Kavita who was a bit annoyed at her daughter but was just speaking out of care for her.

"But mom, I just wanted fluffy." That's what Tanusha called her teddy bear.

"But Tanu, you can always ask me to get it for you. It's dangerous for you to play near the iron box." She said it in an understanding tone as anyone would speak to their little daughter.

"Sorry, mom. I'll not do it again," said Tanusha in a cute apologizing tone that would make any heart melt. Kavita took the teddy bear and picked up her daughter and kissed her on the cheek before giving it to her.

"Tanusha, I need to show you something. Come, let me." Kavita walked to the closet and opened it. Then she took out a beautiful flower-printed dress which was meant for a little girl and said, "Look. Isn't it beautiful? I bought this when I had been to Bangalore last week. I thought I'll surprise you on your birthday but it's so beautiful I couldn't resist." This brought an adorable smile to Tanusha's face and she started insisting that she wanted to wear it right then. Despite many objections by Kavita, she wouldn't relent. Finally, Kavita gave in to her tantrums which would again make anyone's heart melt. She dressed her daughter.

"Awwwhh… This looks so cute on you. Tanu, you look just beautiful in this dress." Tanusha was an adorable child and she looked like the embodiment of all the innocence in the world. Her eyes clearly reflected that.

"See, I was right then," said Tanusha. Kavita smiled and hugged her daughter. This gave Kavita immense happiness and she wanted to keep that mental image of her adorable little daughter right now forever in her mind. A thought worried her that she would grow up soon and have her own life and they may grow to be apart as had happened with her son. This brought tears to Kavita's eyes which were of part happiness and part sorrow. Then she wiped her tears and spoke to her daughter.

"Go now. Show it to papa. Let him see how adorable my daughter looks." Tanusha ran with excitement to go to her papa.

"Arre…Slowlyyy… You'll hurt yourself. Don't run on the stairs."

Tanusha, however, still ran going down the stairs. Kavita just smiled looking at her daughter's excitement.

Tanusha ran downstairs and went to the hall. She called out to her father but he was not to be found in the hall. So she looked for him in the kitchen. But to no avail, he wasn't found there either. Tanusha couldn't control her excitement and she called out 'papa' again but still, there was no answer. Now she gave up and as she decided to go back upstairs, she suddenly heard a voice. It was like someone's crying. A child maybe. She wondered where it was coming from, who it might be.

Now she recognized that the voice was coming from the backside of the house. Probably from Chotu's room, she thought. So she decided to follow it. She slowly went out to the backside veranda of the house. The sobbing voice now became more and more clear to her. It was Chotu who was sobbing. So she went to the door of Chotu's room. The sobbing now became louder to her as she slowly reached the door. The door was closed but not locked. She put her ear to the door to listen more carefully. Now she heard a man's voice too. Probably an adult. When she pressed against the door it opened slightly, and through the narrow gap now opened she looked inside the room. She witnessed a 10-year-old Chotu who was crying. He was made to kneel down in front of a man who had his pants down. It was none other than her father Guru Dutt. He was seen holding the boy's neck and pulling him strongly towards his crotch. The boy was resisting but was no match to the force of the adult. She stayed there watching in shock not knowing what was happening. She was extremely scared. She didn't know what to do. It was a man who she trusted as her beloved father. She could not fathom what was happening and out of fear she opened the door and called out, "Papa."

Dutt immediately pulled up his pants on hearing the voice. He then turned and realized that it was his daughter. He stayed expressionless and stared at her for a moment. Then said, "Tanu,… uh…. What are you doing here?"

"I… I… came to show you my dress." The girl was still confused.

"Oh is it? Gosh… you look beautiful." He was still in his evil space of mind and now seeing his daughter he called out for her, "Come, my dear, Come to papa." It was as if his lust had taken over his sense of thinking now.

Tanusha slowly walked towards her father and as she reached, he hugged her. Then he slowly started undressing her and asked her to kneel down too, while he himself started unzipping his pants and pulled them down once more. When she started crying, he said, "No…No… I'll treat you nicely… Don't cry… don't cry…I'll treat you good…Just trust papa…ok?"

Now Chotu, on the other hand, without knowing what to do tries to save her by hitting him with a stick that he got from nearby. However, that hit didn't seem to hurt him any. But Dutt, angry now, held him by the neck and slapped him in the face. "Bloody piece of shit. How dare you hit me?… Huh…?"

Just right after the moment he hit him and turned back, he saw Kavita by the door which to his mistake he had left open. She stood absolutely shocked.

"What…uhhhh…What are you doing?"

She took a moment to realize what was happening there.

"OH MY GOD… You bloody scoundrel! Are you…? Are you…? Oh my God!" Tears started rolling down her eyes. She came to Tanusha who was half undressed and picked her up. She held Chotu by the arm and started walking towards the main house. She reached the hall and seated both Tanusha and Chotu on the sofa. Both the children were in tears. Kavita started walking up and down the hall holding her hand on her forehead trying to fathom what she had just witnessed. Dutt now came into the hall following them.

"It's not what it looks like."

"Are you kidding me? Then what was that?"

"I'm sorry. I think I have a sickness. You have to trust me."

"A sickness? Really? My God, I don't even know where to start," and she started crying. Dutt came closer to her and tried to hold her hand but she warded it off like the thought of even being touched by him would make her puke.

"Don't. Don't you dare touch me. Just go away."

"Kavita, you need to listen to me."

"I'm not listening to a word you are going to say." She now sat down. "My husband! My own husband doing this! What kind of a father does this to his own child?"

"I've never done this to my Tanu. She just…I don't know…she was just in the wrong place at the wrong time."

"Don't. Just don't. Don't you dare give reasons for what you were doing." She looked at her phone lying on the table. Dutt realized what she was about to do. She went near the table and before she could grab the phone Dutt took it right off the table.

"NO!!" said Dutt.

"You need to give me my phone."

"NO, I don't. What do you think you're doing, huh?"

"I'm going to report to the cops."

"No, you're not."

"Yes. I'm going to. You are a disgusting man and I fucking don't want to see you anymore."

"Please don't. I'm your husband. Please!!!"

"No!!! Don't say that. The fact that you are makes me puke." There was silence for a moment while Kavita realized something.

"Are you…? Are you the one the police are looking for? Oh my God!!! You are the one that Chotu used to talk about. The man in the boiler suit. I can't believe it. My husband!!!!!!"

"Yes. But they don't know that it's me. We need to keep it that way."

"Oh my God!!! How many children have you done this to?"

"That's not the point. I'm going to change. You need to believe me. I'm going to. I just need your help. As I told you, it's my sickness."

"NOOOO…, I'm not going to hear a word out of you. You need to be behind bars." Now, this angered Dutt and he chucked the phone to the ground. Kavita and the children shrieked in fear.

"You need to hear me. And hear me straight. If you inform the cops the whole family's name is going to the ruins. All that you and your family have built. Everything will go to the ruins. What do you think will happen to Tanu, huh? You will just end up spoiling her whole life. She'll be bullied at school and in her life. She will always be known as the daughter of a PEDOPHILE. And do I even need to remind you what's going to happen to your name? You will be tormented for life. Remember you are the one that married the second time and that too with me. The whole village will look upon you with disgusting eyes. They will fucking shame you!! Do you hear me? You hear me, right?"

Kavita now seemed to think for a moment. It was like all he said went right into her mind. She now didn't know what to do. She just collapsed on the sofa sitting and worrying. Dutt now went and tried to lift his daughter lovingly. Tanu went and hugged her mother tightly not letting her go. Kavita said,

"Don't you dare play the loving father now." She lifted Tanu and grabbed Chotu. She now started climbing the stairs to go to her room. Dutt followed them on the stairs and tried to grab Tanusha from Kavita. Kavita didn't let her daughter go. Both Kavita and Dutt now got into a scuffle. In this scuffle, Kavita pushed Dutt with great force and he fell rolling right down the stairs. In this process, he got a hard hit on his head and injured many body parts. Now he lay right down the stairs, on the floor, unconscious without moving. Kavita immediately let her daughter and Chotu go and went down to check Dutt. She tried many times to awaken him but she couldn't. Then she checked his pulse and found that he was still alive. She immediately called for an ambulance.

2020, Rampura, Karnataka

"I couldn't get myself to kill him over the years. Nor did I have the courage to report it to the police. I mean, how could I? It was my and my family's life and reputation that were at stake. But today, that was it." Tears rolled down her eyes, "I guess this is how it was meant to be."

Surya and Rahul had been listening quite intently. Surya still couldn't gather up to talk. So Rahul asked, "What about the murders now in the village?"

"It was me who paid Sathish to do it. I saw the boiler suits and masks in the chemist shop all those years ago shortly after Dutt was admitted to the hospital. There he had also had photos of his victims. He filmed all the assaults on those children and took several photographs too. This sick bastard used to get off on it. So even after selling the shop, I kept the keys to it. After all these years I thought it would be smart to use the suit and the masks and I used to put on the suit and mask whenever I would meet Sathish to order a hit. The cops would be chasing a dead end even if Sathish snitched in any case."

"But why did you kill them? What wrong had they done?" asked Rahul.

"I met Guruji Vishwas a year ago. I was immediately smitten by him. The ideals he thought and the sense of the world he made were something altogether different like never before. He is the one who taught me that we don't have to suffer. Humans aren't meant to be suffering like this. God made us to enjoy His creation of this world. And this is common to all religions. No matter which religion, it teaches that humans are brought upon this world to experience His beautiful creation and any religion that preaches otherwise is completely wrong and misleading. It is we humans who have brought on modifications to every religion to suit the whims and demands of the elite few. Sadly, the world today is run by these people and it has created havoc on this planet. There is suffering for every second, every minute, every hour, and every day on this planet. Guruji preaches that it's not meant to be like this. The only goal of a person suffering now is to reach and be one with God. And Datura or Jimson weed as you call it is one of the pious ways to die and be one with the Almighty. I was the one that brought suffering to these people in their childhood by bringing this beast of a man into this village by marrying him. Somehow, I cannot shake off the fact that I'm responsible for this. Hence, I had to get them killed so that their life scars and the suffering they endured in childhood could be eradicated. You need to understand that they would carry those scars for life. I just set them free. The use of Datura was one pious way of giving up their life. They are one with God now." Kavita was now in complete tears which showed signs of being completely brainwashed. The vulnerable situation she was in after the incident in 2005 and the emotional burden she carried all her life needed a release and it was devastating in the end.

"What about my mother?" asked Surya who had been quiet all this while.

"I'm very sorry about that. She wasn't strong enough to witness you die. She became privy to my plan and when I tried to make her understand that you needed your release from this life and become one with God, she agreed finally but couldn't watch you die while she stayed alive. Maybe that's why she took her own life. But I didn't poison you. I couldn't make myself kill you. You are like my own son and I couldn't do it to a son of mine. Someone got to you before me."

Rahul was now shocked, "You mean you did not poison Surya?"

"No. As I said, I couldn't."

"Then who poisoned him?"

"I really don't know. It was definitely not from my side."

Surya couldn't bear what he was hearing. He shook his head and rubbed his palms across his face. Rahul also still could not come to contemplate what he was hearing. His own mother being a killer and his stepfather being the infamous pedophile in the village. But he continued with disgust, "You didn't even spare your own daughter. You had to poison Tanusha? Huh?"

"But I did not poison her. She took it out of her own will. She was a smart and intelligent girl. Such an innocent soul doesn't deserve a world like this. She was made for something better and she understood that."

"No. You have been consumed by this poison this Guruji has spread. No one in their right mind would do this. You are completely brainwashed," said Rahul. Then he looked over to Surya and said, "Arrest her. Whatever. It doesn't matter to me anymore." He was completely dejected.

But before Surya called for backup to arrest her, she had grabbed the teacup. To her misfortune or fortune, she was stopped by Rahul as he slapped the teacup out of her hand. Her last attempt to practise what she was being brain fed by Guruji went in vain. Now before Surya gathered his phone once again to make the call, his phone rang. It was from his trusted colleague. He picked up the call. He then spoke to his colleague. But Rahul could observe that the speaking was rather less from Surya's side. In fact, as the call went on with time, Surya looked like he became more and more worried. Later Surya hung up and now looked more worried than ever.

"What happened?" asked Rahul.

"There have been mass suicides all over the village. Approximately 20 of Guruji's followers have committed suicide by poisoning." Surya looked dreaded, "There could be more still. Many are admitted to the hospital and are in critical condition."

"What!!!! No, No, NO! THIS CAN'T BE POSSIBLE." Rahul looked at his mother. "What have you people done? What has your Guruji done?"

Kavita just closed her eyes for a moment and then on opening, chanted, "JAI DATURA."

Rahul's phone now started ringing all over the hook. He was being flooded with messages and pings to watch the news. So he said to Surya, "Switch on the television. NOW!!!"

As soon as Surya switched on the television and changed the channel to the news, Rahul and Surya just read the headlines and were shocked. All the channels were broadcasting and covering the same story. Both of them looked like struck by a bolt of lightning. The news said -

"MASS SUICIDES ALL OVER THE STATE OF KARNATAKA BY FOLLOWERS OF A CULT LED BY GURUJI VISHWAS *AKA* INDER KUMAR. THE DEATH TOLL AS OF NOW REACHES 918 MEMBERS."

Rahul exclaimed, "WHAT THE FUCK!!!!!!!!!!!!"

2020, Rampura, Karnataka

Rahul and Surya were overflooded with information over the last two hours. As they were the only people who came to crack the essence and danger the cult was posing, they were visited by the NIA team immediately after the news broke. Even IB officials had communicated with them. This was probably the biggest terror attack in India over the last century. Every agency wanted a piece of them. The media on the other hand was obsessed with the story and wanted to interview both Rahul and Surya. But they were instructed not to do so by the authorities as that could destroy and harm their investigation.

According to the agencies, Guruji had left India on a private jet early that morning which was routed to Kathmandu, Nepal. But to everyone's surprise, the plane strayed off its initial path and was re-routed to Pakistan. According to the Research and Analysis Wing, the plane had landed in Karachi. This was being looked at as a terrorist attack for the same reasons.

Going by the news and the NIA, Guruji Vishwas *aka* Inder Kumar was not listed as a possible terror collaborator. He had been on several trips and was involved in various religious and cult organizations in his life after the untimely death of his wife and the mysterious death of his only daughter. It was later in his life that he started his own cult with its own unique following.

It was being looked like a possible terror attack with the backing and support of the dreaded ISI. The cult received funding from a Pakistani businessman. According to the latest chats intercepted by RAW, it was being concluded that the political brass of China was also celebrating this attack. It was surely a Chinese war tactic and strategy, which says, to win the war without firing a single bullet. Confucius says in his teachings to destroy the enemy without firing even a single bullet and the Communist Party of China follows his ideals strongly. This was probably the biggest terror attack in independent India and all this happened without any weapons of mass destruction and without firing even a single bullet.

Surya and Rahul received an emergency call from the Chief Minister of Karnataka and they were summoned to Bangalore for questioning as they were the only people alive who could shed some light on this incident, as Kavita who got arrested refused to co-operate with the authorities. She just maintained sheer silence. The NIA had also informed Surya and Rahul that they may be summoned by the PM's office and the NSA of India. The chatter in the PM's office described this as the biggest national security threat to India in a long time. The MLA, Sanjay Khadke, has also been detained and grilled for answers.

Surya and Rahul now were on their way to Surya's home to freshen up and pack before they left for Bangalore. Rahul and Surya had insisted that they be left alone to freshen up for some time. The agencies respected their wishes. After all, it had been a tiring and taxing day for both and would probably be a lot of the same in the coming days. The agencies hence understood their need for privacy and left them to pack before they were on their way to Bangalore.

Surya was in his room packing while Rahul had gone to take a shower. Rahul felt the warm water hitting his face with some force. It had been three days since he showered and no one would blame him for that. His life had been turned upside down since he came to Rampura. While in the shower Rahul began to contemplate and think about what had happened in the last few days. The killings orchestrated by his mother, the pedophile of a stepfather, the death of Sharda, the poisoning of Surya, the death of Sathish, his sister being poisoned who by the way had recovered well over the last few hours, and to top it all the mass suicide of 918 people. Rahul began to go over all these events again and again in his head. The more he thought about this, he realized that Guruji could not have managed this without a strong General to implement his plans. But who was the General? This question remained unanswered. And also something that remained unanswered was who poisoned Surya and who killed Sathish, as Sathish was the only link to stop the alleged terror attack.

The more he thought about it, a faint idea of the person behind all these came to his mind. Later as he thought of the common link between all these events, he began to get a good idea of the person who might be behind this. He got an idea of the person who might be Guruji's General. But that was too far-fetched and impossible. So he came out of the shower with his towel wrapped around his waist and called out to Surya to discuss his ideas. Rahul went over to the balcony looking for Surya. Surya wasn't on the balcony. But Rahul stood at the railing near the balcony and started staring at the village standing there. It was a calm atmosphere he needed most right now and that was what he got standing on the balcony overlooking the village. After a brief moment, he turned back. To his utter shock, he found Surya behind him wearing an orange robe and black wristbands made of cotton cloth. Surya had a gun pointed towards Rahul's forehead. Suddenly, Rahul started to realize how he was being played.

"Surya? Did you…?" Rahul was cut short by a bullet straight through his forehead. The gunshot had no sound as a silencer was used. Rahul fell to the ground from the balcony immediately and a pool of blood started coming out of his head.

Later, Surya looked at his Bangalore-to-London flight ticket and his passport. Then he took another flight ticket out of his pocket which was from London to Karachi. But this time under a different name and different passport. The passport was a fake one of Pakistani origin and the name read HAMID GUL.

The END